LIZ FIELDING

Reunited: Marriage in a Million

SecretsWeKeep

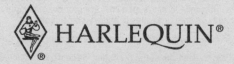

HARLEQUIN®

TORONTO • NEW YORK • LONDON
AMSTERDAM • PARIS • SYDNEY • HAMBURG
STOCKHOLM • ATHENS • TOKYO • MILAN • MADRID
PRAGUE • WARSAW • BUDAPEST • AUCKLAND

ISBN-13: 978-0-373-03970-8
ISBN-10:   0-373-03970-0

REUNITED: MARRIAGE IN A MILLION

First North American Publication 2007.

Copyright © 2007 by Liz Fielding.

Printed in U.S.A.

Belle, unable to say another word, simply raised her trophy in acknowledgment of the applause. In front of her was a sea of faces, but there was only one that would have made this moment memorable. Her husband's.

And as if the need, so powerful, called up the man, she saw Ivo standing by the door, looking at her. The only person in the room not smiling. Not applauding.

She walked down the steps and, ignoring the outstretched hands, walked toward him until the applause died away to silence and she was close enough to touch him.

Not an illusion conjured up out of her need, but real, solid.

He wasn't in evening dress. Fine rain misted his hair, the shoulders of his long overcoat, and belatedly she realized that he hadn't turned up to witness her big moment. That he was here because there was something wrong.

Dear Reader,

Writing, by its very nature, is a solitary business, and so it was a very special pleasure to collaborate with two of my favorite authors on the trilogy SECRETS WE KEEP.

The plan was to find a moment in time when the lives of three women touched, a moment that would change them forever, and brainstorming sessions burned up cyberspace as we bounced ideas around about how Belle, Simone and Claire would meet. What common theme in their lives had drawn them together, made them so instantly empathetic?

Join them as, high in the Himalayas, raising money for charity on a sponsored cycle ride, they spill out their secrets and pledge each other support and friendship. And follow Belle home as she challenges herself to renew her life and put right a mistake that has haunted her—and discovers that the man she loves is, truly, a man in a million.

With love,

Liz

SecretsWeKeep

*Share the love and laughter with three friends—
on their journey to wedded bliss...*

In the breathtaking peaks of the Himalayas,
three women on the most challenging cycling
adventure of their lives are about to
share the secrets of their hearts.

They make a pact to change their lives,
and when the trip comes to an end and the
three new friends head home to different corners
of the globe, Belle, Simone and Claire
start to take charge of their destinies....

Meet the men who will share their secrets and
bring love and laughter to the lives of these
extraordinary women.

August—*Liz Fielding*
REUNITED: MARRIAGE IN A MILLION

September—*Barbara Hannay*
NEEDED: HER MR. RIGHT

October—*Jackie Braun*
FOUND: HER LONG-LOST HUSBAND

For Barb and Jackie, my companions,
on the journey—it was a joy working with you.
And for Liz and Gil, who did the actual pedaling.

PROLOGUE

'THE car is here. Your paparazzi army are forming their usual guard of honour.'

Ivo was waiting, his face expressionless. Waiting for her to back down, tell him that she wouldn't go, and Belle had to fight back the treacherous sting of tears.

She didn't cry, ever.

Why couldn't he understand? Why couldn't he see that she hadn't chosen to spend twelve days cycling over the Himalayas on some whim?

This was important to her. Something she needed to do.

By demanding she drop out at a moment's notice to play hostess at one of his power-broking weekends at his country house in Norfolk, he was making it plain that nothing—not her career, certainly not some charity stunt—was as important as being his wife.

That he had first call on her.

If only she could have told him, explained. But if she'd done that, he wouldn't want her to stay...

'I have to go,' she said.

For a moment she thought he was going to say something, but instead he nodded, picked up the heavy rucksack that contained everything she would need for the next three weeks and reached for the door handle.

By the time the door was open, Belle was wearing a smile for the cameras. She paused briefly on the step with Ivo at her side, then they made their way to the car.

The chauffeur took the rucksack and, while he was stowing it, Ivo took her hand, looked down at her with grave eyes that never betrayed what he was thinking.

'Look after yourself.'

'Ivo…' She stopped herself from begging him to come to the airport with her. 'I'll be passing through Hong Kong on my way home. If you happened to find you had some business there, maybe we could take a few days…'

He made no comment—he never made promises he could not keep—but simply kissed her cheek, helped her into the car, repeating his directive to 'take care' before closing the door. She turned as the car pulled away, but he was already striding up the steps to the house, wanting to get back to work.

The chauffeur stopped at the airport drop-off point, loaded her bag on to a trolley, wished her good luck, and then she was alone. Not alone, as a woman with a loving husband waiting at home might feel.

Just…alone.

CHAPTER ONE

'...So THAT'S it for Day Nine of the Great Cycling Adventure. Tomorrow I'm told it's going to be "a gentle, undulating rise"...' Belle Davenport wiped away a trickle of sweat on her sleeve and smiled into the camera. *'These guys really have a sense of humour. If seeing me sweating and in pain in a good cause is making you feel good, feel bad, feel anything, please remember any donation you make, no matter how small, will make a real difference...'*

Belle Davenport wrapped up for the camera, hit send and, as soon as she'd got a reply confirming it had been safely received, unplugged her satellite phone. It was only then that she realised that what she had thought was sweat was, in fact, blood.

'You do know that he brought you down quite deliberately.' Claire Mayfield, an American sharing her tent, as well as her pain, was outraged.

'He helped me up again,' Belle pointed out.

'Only after he'd taken pictures. You should make a complaint to the organisers. You could have been seriously hurt.'

'No whining allowed,' she said, then winced as Simone Gray—the third member of their group—having cleaned up the graze on her forehead, started to work on her grazed thigh.

'Sorry...nearly done.' Then, tossing the wipe away and applying a dressing, said, 'In this world, Claire, it isn't enough for the media that you're putting yourself through seven kinds of torture to raise money for street kids. They want you down in the dirt too.' Simone was executive editor of an Australian women's magazine. She knew what she was talking about.

'Glamour, excitement, sleazebags with cameras waiting to catch you with your face in the mud,' Belle confirmed, with a wry smile.

'In London, okay,' Claire persisted. Then, 'Actually, it's not okay, but I suppose in your business you learn to live with the intrusion. But halfway up the Himalayas?'

'Are we only halfway up? It feels higher.' Then, shaking her head, Belle said, 'Simone's right, Claire. It's all part of the game. No complaints. I've been at the top of my particular tree for a long time. I guess it's my turn to be set up as an Aunt Sally and knocked off.'

'Set up?'

'Put in a position where not to do it would have made me look mean-spirited, all mouth and no trousers, so to speak. The kind of television personality who encourages others to do the hard work while she sits back on the breakfast telly sofa, flashing her teeth and as much cleavage as the network can get away with at that time in the morning.'

'You're not like that.'

'No?'

'No!'

Belle had gone for 'arch', but found herself profoundly touched by Claire's belief in her.

'Well, maybe not this time,' she admitted, smiling to herself as she remembered just how easy it had been to manipulate the people who thought they were pulling the strings. 'It's amazing how far acting dumb will get you.'

'So...what? You really wanted to come?'

'Shh!' She lifted a finger to her lips. 'The walls of tents have ears.' She grinned. 'All it took was, "If we sent someone for this charity cycle ride it would make a great feature. Lots of opportunities to address a real problem. Get the public to join in with sponsorship." An idle, "Who could we send?", accompanied by just the tiniest shiver of horror at the thought, for the director to get ideas about how much the media would enjoy seeing me getting sweaty and dirty on a bike. The publicity it would generate. Got to think of those ratings…'

For Belle the pain was well worth the extra publicity it would generate for a cause dear to her heart, enabling her to support it publicly without raising any questions about why she cared so much.

Knowing that she was the one pulling the strings didn't take the sting out of her thigh, though. And out here, in the rarefied air of the mountains, spending her time with people who'd financed themselves, who were doing it without any of the publicity circus that inevitably surrounded a breakfast show queen putting herself at the sharp end of fund raising, she was beginning to feel like a fraud. The kind of celebrity who'd do anything to stay in the spotlight, the kind of woman who'd put up with anything to stay in a hollow marriage, because without them she'd be nothing.

She pushed away the thought and said, 'If you think this is about the children, rather than ratings, Claire, you are seriously overestimating the moral probity of breakfast television.'

It was the ratings grabbing report-to-camera straight from the day's ride—the never-less-than-immaculate Belle Davenport reduced to a dishevelled, sweaty puddle—that the company wanted and the media were undoubtedly relishing. Why else would they have sponsored one of their own to come along and take pictures? But after a week it seemed that honest sweat had got old; now they wanted blood and tears too.

Today they'd got the blood and no doubt that was the image that would be plastered over tomorrow's front pages and, when she got home, she'd shame them into a very large donation to her cause for that.

No way in hell were they going to get her tears.

She did not cry.

'That's…' Claire grinned. 'That's actually pretty smart.'

'It takes more than blonde hair and a well-developed chest to stay at the top in television,' Simone pointed out. Then, regarding her thoughtfully, she went on, 'So the street kids get the money, the spotlight on their plight, the television company get the ratings. What are you getting out of it, Belle?'

'Me?'

'You could have stayed at home, squeezing your viewers heartstrings, but you wanted to come yourself. You must have had a reason.'

'Apart from getting myself all over the newspapers looking like this?'

'You don't need publicity.'

'Everyone needs publicity,' she said, but her laughter had a hollow ring and neither of her two companions joined in. 'No, well, maybe I just wanted to feel good about myself. Isn't that why everyone does this kind of stunt?'

'If that's the plan,' Claire said, lying back on her bedroll with a groan, 'it isn't working. All I feel is sore.'

'Maybe the feeling good part kicks in later,' Belle replied sympathetically.

She knew she hadn't been the only one who'd gone through a three-ring circus to get here. No matter how much she hated it, she understood that even when the redtops had people digging in your dustbin for dirt they could use, it wasn't personal.

For Claire, though, a pampered princess with a token job working in her father's empire, the sniggering criticism had been just that. Deeply personal.

What the hell; they'd shown them. With a determined attempt at brightness, Belle continued, 'In the meantime I've lost weight, improved my muscle tone, gained some blisters...'

'No.'

She gave up on the distraction of her newly-defined calf muscles and caught something—a bleakness to Simone's expression that was new.

'What *have* you got out of this?' she demanded. 'Seriously.'

'Seriously?' She looked from Simone to Claire and realised

they were both regarding her with a sudden intensity, that the atmosphere in the tent had shifted. Darkened.

'Seriously.' Belle took a deep breath. 'Seriously' meant confronting the truth. 'Seriously' meant having to do something about it. But, forget the publicity, forget the cameras—that was what this trip had been all about. Stepping out of her comfort zone. Putting herself out there. Doing something real. Except she wasn't, not really. She was still hiding. From the world. From her husband. Most of all from herself.

'You can see so far up here,' Belle began uncertainly. Not quite sure what she was going to say. Where this was going. 'When we stopped for that drinks break this afternoon, I looked back and you could see the road we'd travelled winding all the way back down to the valley.'

She faced the rangy Australian, the petite American, who shared her tent. They'd tended each other's grazes, rubbed liniment into each other's aching muscles, they'd eaten together, battling with chopsticks while vowing never to travel again without a fork in their rucksack. They'd laughed, ridden alongside each other since they'd found themselves sharing a cab from the airport to the hotel when they'd first arrived, each of them scared in a what-the-hell-am-I-doing-here? way, yet excited by the challenge they were facing. Outwardly, they were women who had everything and yet they'd seemed to recognise something in each other, some hidden need.

Instant soul mates, they had become true friends.

It was a new experience for Belle. She'd never had girl-friends. Not as a kid, struggling to survive, not in the care home, certainly not in the stab-in-the-back atmosphere of daytime television.

The media bosses, the tabloid hacks, the gossip mags, all used her to lift circulation in a way that made her sister-in-law curl her lips in disdain. And her husband, money-machine tycoon Ivo Grenville, whose eyes burned with lust—the only thing he was unable to control—despised himself for wanting her so much that he'd committed the ultimate sacrifice and married her.

None of them bothered to look deeper than the 'blonde bombshell' image that she'd fallen into by accident, to find out who she really was. Not that she blamed them. She wore her image like a sugar-coated veneer; only she knew how thin it was.

These two women, total strangers when they'd met a couple of weeks earlier, knew her better than most, had seen her at her most vulnerable, had shared their lives with her. All of them, on the surface, had everything; Claire was the daughter of one of the world's wealthiest men and Simone had risen to the top in a very tough business. But outward appearances could be deceptive. She'd been trusted with glimpses into their lives that few people had seen, which was why she knew that Claire and Simone would understand what she'd felt when she'd looked back down the road.

It was steep, hard going, and all the twists and turns were laid out before her—a metaphor for her life. Then, before the threatening crack became unstoppable, she let it go and said, 'How many more days is this torture going to last?'

'Three,' Simone said quickly, apparently as anxious as she was to step back from a yawning chasm that had opened up in front of them.

'Three? Can I survive three more days without a decent bed, clean sheets?' Claire asked.

'Without a hot bath.'

'Without a manicure,' Belle added, apparently intent on examining her nails, but she was more interested in Simone's obvious relief that the moment of introspection that she herself had provoked had been safely navigated. Then, because actually her nails did look terrible, 'I'm going to have to have extensions,' she sighed.

Normally long, painted, perfect, she'd trimmed them short for the ride, but now they were cracked, dry, ingrained with dirt that no amount of cold water would shift. As she looked at them, dark memories stirred and she curled her fingers into her palm, out of sight.

'What's the first thing you'll do when we hit that hotel in Hong Kong?' she asked.

'After I've run a hot bath?' Claire grinned. 'Call room service and order smoked salmon, half a ton of watercress served with dark rye bread cut wafer-thin and spread with fresh butter.' Then, as an afterthought, 'And chocolate fudge cake.'

'I'll go along with that and raise you ice-cold champagne,' Belle added, grinning.

'The champagne sounds good,' Simone said, 'but I vote we pass on the healthy stuff and go straight for the chocolate fudge cake.'

'White chocolate fudge cake,' Belle said. 'And a hot tub to sit in while we eat it.'

'Er…that's a great idea,' Claire said, 'but won't your husband have ideas of his own in the hot tub department?'

'Ivo?' Belle found herself struggling to keep the smile going. 'He *is* coming to meet you?'

For a moment she allowed herself that fantasy; that she'd reach the end of the journey and he'd be there, scooping her up into his arms. Carrying her off to a luxury suite to make hot sweet love to her.

With the slightest shake of her head, she said, 'No.' About to make some excuse for him—pressure of business was always a safe one—she found she couldn't do it. 'To tell you the truth,' she said, 'I'm in the marital doghouse.' With the smallest gesture she took in their cramped surroundings. 'He didn't want me to do this.'

'You're kidding?' Claire frowned. 'I thought he was so supportive. I've seen pictures of you guys in those lifestyle magazines. The way he looks at you. The way it reads, you have the perfect marriage.'

'You mean captions like… "Breakfast television's bombshell, Belle Davenport, ravishing in Valentino, arriving at a royal gala last night with her millionaire businessman husband, Ivo Grenville."?'

They always printed one of her arriving—that moment when she leaned forward as Ivo helped her from the car. The one that never failed to catch the look of a man who couldn't wait to get her home again, feeding the fantasy that had grown around them after their 'couldn't wait' runaway marriage on a tropical island.

At least the looks were real enough. His desire was the one thing she'd never doubted. As for the rest...

'I'm sorry to disappoint you, but I'm the original one hundred per cent genuine trophy wife.' The bitter words spilled out of her before she could stop them. The only difference was that he hadn't dumped a long-serving first wife for her; on the contrary, she was the one who'd be dumped when he wanted a proper wife. The kind you had kids and grew old with. 'He was throwing a shooting party last weekend on his estate in Norfolk. A business thing. He wanted me on show. The hostess with the mostest.' She pulled a face. 'I don't have to explain what I've got the most of, do I?' she said as, hand behind her head, she leaned forward, giving the girls a mock cupcake cleavage pose.

'You've got a lot more than that,' Simone chipped in. 'Holding down a job in television takes a lot more than a perfect pair of D cups. And the kind of party you're talking about takes a serious amount of organising.'

'Not by me.'

Her sister-in-law, Ivo's live-in social secretary and a woman with more breeding than a pedigree chum, handled all that. But then she had been born to it. Benenden, finishing school in Switzerland, the statutory Cordon Bleu, Constance Spry courses for the girls-in-pearls debutantes. Another world...

'I'm just there for display purposes to show his business competitors that there isn't a thing they can do that he can't do better.'

'Oh, Belle...' Claire seemed lost for words.

Simone was more direct. 'If that's all there is to your marriage, Belle, why do you stay with him?'

'Honestly?' They were high in the Himalayas, the air was stingingly cold, clear, cleaner than anything she'd ever known. Anything but the truth would pollute it. 'For the security. The safety. The knowledge that, married to him, I'll never be hungry or cold or frightened ever again...'

The truth, but not the whole truth. Passion, security, she would admit to. Falling in love with him had been the mistake...

'But you're bright, successful in your own right—'

'Am I?' She shrugged. 'From the outside I suppose it looks like that, but every day of my life I expect someone to find me out, expose me as a fraud…' Simone made a tiny sound, almost of distress, but shook her head quickly as Belle frowned. 'Let's face it, there's no one as unemployable as a past-her-sell-by-date breakfast television host.' Even as she said it, she knew that she was just making excuses. She was not extravagant and with Ivo's skilful investment of her money, the only thing she truly needed from him was the one commodity he was unable to give. Himself.

There was an emotional vacuum at the heart of her life that had started long before she'd met him. He was not the only one incapable of making a wholehearted commitment to their partnership. She was equally to blame and now it was time to call it a day. Make the break. Let him go.

She'd known it for a long time, just hadn't had the courage to admit it, face up to what that would mean.

'If you want the unadorned truth,' she said, 'I hate my career, I hate my marriage—'

Not that she blamed Ivo for that. He was trapped by his hormones in exactly the same way that she was trapped by her own pitiful fears. They were, it occurred to her, very bad for each other.

'In fact, when it comes right down to it, I hate my life.' She thought about it. 'No, scrub that. I guess I just hate myself—'

'Belle, honey…'

As they reached out to offer some kind of comfort, she shook her head, not wanting it. Not deserving it from these special women. 'I've got a sister somewhere, back there. Lost on the road.' She didn't have to explain. She knew they'd understand that she wasn't talking about the road they were travelling together, but the one leading back to the past. 'I haven't seen her since she was four years old.'

'Four?' Claire frowned. 'What happened to her? Did your family split up?'

'Family?' She gave a short laugh. 'I'm not like you…' She sucked in her breath, trying to hold back the words. Then, slowly she finished the sentence. 'I'm not like you, Claire.' She glanced at Simone, who was unusually quiet, and on an impulse she reached out, laid a hand over hers. 'Or Simone.' Then, lifting her chin a little. 'We're here to raise money for street kids, right? Well, that was me. It's why I made such a big thing of this fund raiser. Why I'm here.' Feeling exposed in the way an alcoholic must feel the first time he admitted he had a problem, she said, 'My real name is Belinda Porter and I was once a street kid.'

She'd never told anyone where she'd come from. Anything about herself. On the contrary, she'd done everything she could to scrub it out of her mind. Not even Ivo knew. He'd had the tidied-up fairy story version of her life: the one with kindly foster parents—who she'd conveniently killed off in a tragic car accident— a business course at the local college—not the straight from school dead-end job in a call centre. Only the lucky break of being drafted in to work the phones on the biggest national fund raising telethon had been true, but then she'd been 'discovered' live on air; everyone knew that story.

How could she blame him for a lack of emotional commitment to her when she had kept most of her life hidden from him? A husband deserved more than that.

She swallowed. 'My mother, my sister, the three of us begged just to live,' she said. 'Exactly like the children we're here to help.'

For a moment no one spoke.

Then Claire said, 'What happened to her, Belle? Your sister.'

That was it? No shrinking away in horror? Just compassion? Concern…?

She shook her head. 'Nothing. Nothing bad. Our mother died.' She shook her head. That was a nightmare she'd spent years trying to erase. 'Social Services did their best, but looking back it's obvious that I was the kind of teenage girl who gives decent women nightmares. Our mother was protective, would have fought off a tiger to keep us from harm, from the danger out there, but I'd seen too much, knew too much. I was trouble just waiting to happen. Daisy was still young enough to adapt. And she was so pretty. White-blonde curls, blue eyes. Doll-like, you know? A social worker laid it out for me. It was too late for me but, given a chance, she could have a real family life.'

'That must have hurt so much.'

She looked up, grateful for Claire's intuitive understanding of just how painful it had been to be unwanted.

'It's odd,' she said, 'because I was the one named after a doll. Belinda. Maybe it was some need in her to reach back to a time of innocence, hope.' She shook her head. 'It never suited me. I was never that kind of little girl.'

'You have the blonde hair.'

'Bless you, Claire,' she said with a grin, 'but this particular shade of blonde is courtesy of a Knightsbridge crimper who charges telephone numbers. She pulled on a strand, made a face. He's going to have a fit when he sees the state of it.'

She reached for the sewing kit. There was no hairdresser here and no wardrobe department to produce a clean, fresh pair of trousers for the morning. If she didn't stitch up the tear, her thigh would be flapping in the wind.

'Daisy was different,' she said, concentrating on threading a needle. 'I hated her so much for being able to smile at the drop of a hat. Smile so that people would want to mother her, love her.' Her hands were shaking too much and she gave up on the needle. 'I hated her so much that I let someone walk away with her, adopt her, turned my back on her. Lost her.'

'I lost someone, too.'

Claire, suddenly the focus of their attention, gave an awkward little shrug. 'It must be this place, or maybe it's just that here life is pared down to the basics. The next marker, the next drink of water, the next meal. Meeting with the people who exist here on the bare essentials.' She took Belle's needle, threaded it, began to work on the torn trousers. 'There are no distractions, none of the day-to-day white noise of life to block out stuff you'd rather not think about and with nothing else to keep it occupied, the mind throws up stuff you've put in your memory's deep storage facility. Not wanted in this life.'

'Who did you lose, Claire?' Simone, pale beneath the tan that no amount of sun screen could entirely block in the thin air, almost whispered the words.

'My husband. Ethan. A decent, hard-working man…'

'I had no idea you'd been married,' Belle said.

Claire looked at her ringless hand, flexed her fingers, then with a little shiver said, 'As far as the world is concerned, it never happened. One messy little marriage discreetly dissolved with a stroke of a lawyer's pen.'

'It can't have been that simple.'

'Oh, you'd be surprised just how simple money can make things.' Then, 'In my defence, I was twenty-one years old and desperate to get away from my father. He isn't that easy to escape. He paid my husband to disappear and I was weak, I let him.'

'Twenty-one? You were practically a kid.'

Claire lifted her head, straightened her back. 'Old enough to have known better. To have been stronger.' Then, 'He's been on my mind a lot lately. Ethan. I guess it's all part of this.' Her gesture took in the tent, their surroundings. 'I work for my father, but as far as the rest of his staff are concerned I'm a joke, a pampered princess with a make-work job whose only concern is the next manicure, the latest pair of designer shoes. I came on this charity ride to shake up that image, to prove, to myself at least, that I'm better than that.'

'And finding Ethan would help?' Belle asked. 'He did take the money and run,' she pointed out.

'Why wouldn't he? I didn't do anything, say anything to stop him.' She shook her head. 'It would undermine a man's confidence, something like that, don't you think? I need to find him, make sure that he's all right.' She swallowed. 'More than that. I need him to forgive me. If he can find it in his heart to do that, then maybe I'll be able to forgive myself.'

Simone, who'd been increasingly quiet, covered her mouth with her hand to stifle a moan. 'Forgive yourself? Who will forgive me?' As Claire, all concern, reached out to her, took her hand, a sob escaped her and then it all came pouring out of her, like a breached dam. A story so terrible that it made Belle's own loss seem almost bearable.

For a heartbeat, after she'd finished her story, there was total silence as Simone waited, her eyes anticipating horrified rejection. As one, Belle and Claire put their arms around her, held her.

'I can't believe I told you that,' she said finally, when she could speak. 'I can't believe you still want to know me.'

'I can't believe you've kept it bottled up for so long,' Claire said tenderly.

'Some secrets are so bad that it takes something special for us to be able to find the words,' Belle said quietly. 'It seems that each of us needs to walk back a way, make our peace with the past.'

'This journey we're on isn't going to be over when we fall into a hot bath, crawl between clean sheets, is it?' Claire whispered. 'This has just been the beginning.'

'The easy bit.' Belle swallowed, feeling a little as if she'd just stepped off the edge of a precipice.

'But at least we won't be alone. We'll have each other.'

'Will we? You'll be home in America, Simone will be back in Australia and I'll be in England, looking for Daisy. She could be anywhere.' Then, 'I could be anywhere.'

Belle closed her eyes and for a moment the fear was so great that all she wanted to do was turn the clock back to the second before she stopped on the road and looked back. If she just kept facing forward, moving forward, she wouldn't see the demons snapping at her heels. Then, as if sensing her fear, Claire took one of her hands, Simone the other.

'It's not just Daisy I have to find,' she said, turning her hands to grasp them. 'I've been living behind this image for so long that I'm not sure who I am any more. I need to be on my own. To get away from all the pretence.'

'Belle…' Simone regarded her with concern. 'Don't do anything rash. Ivo could help you.'

She shook her head.

'I've used him as a prop for long enough. Some journeys you have to take alone.'

'Not alone,' Claire quickly assured her. 'You'll have us.'

'If you have to do this, Belle, we'll be there for you.' Simone straightened. 'For each other. Support, encouragement, a cyber-shoulder to cry on and with three time-zones we'll have 24/7 coverage!'

They both looked to Belle and the three of them clasped hands, too choked to speak.

Belle hadn't told anyone when to expect her. If she'd phoned ahead, the television company would have sent a car or Ivo's sister would have despatched the chauffeur to pick her up. But having made the decision to cut her ties with both marriage and job, it seemed hypocritical to use either of them.

Or maybe just stupid, she thought as she abandoned the endless queue for taxis and headed down into the underground to catch a train into London.

She'd have to turn up for work until her contract expired at the end of the month.

She pulled a face at this reminder that her agent—right now pulling out all the stops as he negotiated a new contract for her— was someone else she was going to have to face…who was never going to understand.

She wasn't sure she understood herself. It had all seemed so clear up in the mountains, so simple when she'd made that life-changing pact with Claire and Simone and they'd sealed it with their last bar of chocolate.

Back in London, faced with reality, she felt very alone and she shivered as, with a rush of air, the train pulled in to the station.

She climbed aboard, settled into a corner and automatically took out a book to avoid direct eye contact with the passengers opposite. Scarcely necessary. Who would recognise her, bundled up against the raw November chill, no make-up, her hair covered in a scarf twisted around like a turban to disguise the damage wrought by six weeks without the attention of her stylist?

How easily one slid from instantly recognisable celebrity to some woman no one would glance at twice on the underground.

Without the constant attention of those people whose job it was to polish her appearance, the lifestyle magazines, the safety net of her marriage, her career, who would she be?

What would it take for her to fall right off the face of civilisation, the way her mother had? One bad decision, one wrong turning and she, too, could be spiralling downward…

Fear crawled over her, prickling her skin, bringing her out in a cold sweat, and an urge to abandon all her grand ideals, crawl back into the comfort zone of the life she had and be grateful for it, overwhelmed her.

Daisy didn't need her.

In all likelihood she'd forgotten she even existed. What would be the point of selfishly blundering in, disturbing her doubtless perfect life with memories they'd all rather bury, just to ease her own conscience?

Wouldn't the selfless thing be to trace her, find out what she needed and help her anonymously, from a distance, the way she had always supported charities that helped street kids?

Daisy was nineteen, at university in all likelihood. She'd probably die of embarrassment to be confronted by a sister whose success was due solely to the size of her bosom, the huskiness in her voice.

Worse, once the press found out about her sister—and it was inevitable that they would—they'd keep digging until they had it all.

No teenager needed that and there were other ways to redeem herself. Daisy would need somewhere to live. She could fix that for her somehow. Ivo would know…

She caught herself.

Not Ivo. Her. She'd find out.

She exited from the underground station to the relative peace of Saturday morning in the capital before the shops had opened and was immediately confronted by a man selling *The Big Issue*—the badge of the homeless. She fought, as she always had to, the desperate urge to run away and instead forced herself to stand, take out the money to buy a copy of the magazine, shake her head when he offered her change. Wish him good luck before hailing a passing black cab and making her escape. Pushing away the thought that she could have done more.

The driver nodded as she leaned in to give her address. 'Welcome back, Miss Davenport.'

The immediate recognition was a balm, warming her, making her feel safe. 'The disguise isn't working, then?' she said, relaxing into a smile.

'You'd have to wear a paper bag over your head, miss.' Then, when she'd given him her address, climbed in the back, 'The missus'll be chuffed when I tell her I had you in the back. She's been following your bike ride. Sponsored you herself.'

'How kind. What's her name?'

She made a mental note so that she could mention her donation when she went back on air on Monday, chatted for a few minutes, then fished the cellphone out of her pocket and turned it on.

It hunted for a local network, then beeped, warning her that she had seventeen new messages.

'Please call…' from her agent.

'Please call…' from the director of her show. 'Please call… Please call…' The reassuring template messages of her life. And, just like that, the fear, never far below the surface, dissipated.

Smiling, she flicked the button to next and found herself reading, 'I wish you were my sister, Belle. Good luck. Hugs.' Not a template message, not business, but a 'care' message from Claire, sent before she'd boarded her own plane back to the States.

The next, from Simone, said, 'Are you as scared as me?' Scared? Simone? Brilliant, successful, practically perfect Simone who, like her, like Claire, had a dark secret that haunted her.

She'd left them in the departure lounge at the airport in Hong Kong and it had felt as if she was tearing off an arm to leave them. And now they'd reached out and touched her just at the point at which her resolve was on the point of crumbling. For a moment she was too shaken to move.

'We're here, Miss Davenport,' the driver said and she looked up, realised that the cab had stopped.

'One moment.' She quickly thumbed in her reply to Claire. 'I wish you were, too!'. True. If Claire were her sister she wouldn't be faced with this.

To Simone she began, 'We don't have to do this…' Except that wasn't what Simone wanted from her. What they'd all signed up to. She wanted, deserved, encouragement, the mutual support they'd promised each other. Not permission to bottle out at the first faint-heart moment from someone who was looking for an excuse to do the same.

A week ago in the clear, clean air of the Himalayas, in the company of two women who, for the first time in her adult life she'd been able to open up to, confide in, be totally honest with, she'd felt as if she'd seen a glimpse of something rare, something special that could be hers if only she had the courage to reach for it.

The minute she'd set foot in London, all the horrors of her childhood seemed to reach out from the pavement to grab at her, haul her back where she belonged and, terrified, she couldn't wait to scuttle back into the safety of her gilded cage, pulling the door shut behind her.

She looked at the phone and realised that whatever message she sent now, fight or flee, would set the course of the rest of her life.

She closed her eyes, put herself back in the place she'd been a few days ago, then wrote a new message.

'Scared witless, but we can do this.' And hit send.

A fine sentiment, she thought as she climbed from the cab and stood, clutching her rucksack, outside the Belgravia town house that had been her husband's family home for generations.

Now all she had to do was prove it.

CHAPTER TWO

BELLE walked through the open front door and, if her heart could have sunk any lower, the view through the dining room doors to the chaos of caterers and florists in full cry would have sent it to her boots. She'd arrived in the middle of preparations for one of Ivo's power-broking dinners that her sister-in-law would be directing with the same concentration and attention to detail as a five-star general planning a campaign.

About to toss in the proverbial hand grenade, she kept her head down and headed straight for the library, where she knew she'd find her husband.

The fact that it was barely past nine o'clock on a Saturday morning made no difference to Ivo Grenville, only that he'd be working at home rather than at his office.

He didn't look up as she opened the door, giving her a precious few seconds to look at him, imprint the memory.

One elbow was propped on the desk, his forehead resting on long fingers, his world reduced to the document in front of him.

He had this ability to focus totally on one thing to the exclusion of everything else, whether it was acquiring a new company, a conversation in the lift with his lowliest employee, making love to his wife. He did everything with the same attention to detail, intensity, perfectionism. If, just once, he'd cracked, had an off-day like the rest of the human race, seemed *fallible* . . .

The ache in her throat intensified as, with a pang of tenderness she saw the dark hollows at his temple, a touch of silver that she hadn't noticed before threaded through the thick cowlick of dark hair that slid across his hand. He was tired, she thought. He drove himself too hard, working hours that would be considered inhuman if he'd expected his staff to emulate him, and she longed to be able to just go to him, put her arms around him, silently soothe away the stress…

Just be a wife.

He dragged his hand down over his face, long fingers pinching the bridge of his nose as, eyes closed, he gathered himself to continue.

Then, maybe remembering the sound of the door opening, he looked up and caught her flat-footed, without her defences in place.

'Belle?' He rose slowly to his feet, saying her name as if he couldn't believe it was her. Not that surprising. He'd never seen her looking like this before. The advantage of not sharing a bedroom with her husband was that he never saw her with morning hair, skin crumpled from a night with her face in a pillow. Definitely not in clothes she'd been travelling in for the better part of twenty-four hours, with nothing on her face to hide behind but a thin film of moisturiser. It was little wonder that for a moment he appeared uncharacteristically lost. 'I didn't expect you until tomorrow.'

Not exactly an accusation of thoughtlessness, but a very long way from expressing delight that she was home a day early.

'I switched to an earlier flight.'

'How did you get from the airport?' That was all the time it took him to gather himself, concentrate on the practicalities. 'If you'd called, Miranda would have sent the car.'

Not him, but his ever present, ever helpful little sister. Always there. As focused and perfect as Ivo himself. Too rich to have to bother with building a career, she was simply marking time until some man—heaven help him—who met her requirements in breeding, who was her equal in wealth, realised that she would make the perfect wife.

It was Miranda, not her, who was the chatelaine here, running her brother's social diary and his house with pinpoint precision. The person the staff looked to for their orders.

Who'd had a separate suite ready for her when they'd returned from their honeymoon so that her 4:00 a.m. starts wouldn't disturb Ivo.

That was the inviolable rule of the house. Nothing must be allowed to disturb Ivo.

Not even his wife.

Little wonder, Belle thought, that she'd always felt more like a guest here. Tolerated for the one thing she could give him that not even the most brilliant sister could deliver.

Even now she had to fight the programmed need to apologise for her lapse of good manners in arriving before she was expected. The truth was that she hadn't rung to tell Ivo the change to her schedule because to call would be to hope that just this once he'd drive down to Heathrow himself, join the crowd of eager husbands and wives waiting for that first glimpse of a loved one as they spilled out into the arrivals hall. Just as she'd hoped that he would, despite what she'd told Claire and Simone, fly to Hong Kong to meet her.

Her heart just wouldn't quit hoping.

But his momentary lapse from absolute certainty had given her the necessary few seconds to gather herself, restore the protective shell she wore to disguise her true feelings, and she was able to shrug and say, 'It seemed less bother to get the train. No,' she said quickly, as he finally abandoned his papers, stopping him before he could touch her, kiss her. 'I've been travelling for twenty-four hours. I'm not fit to be touched.'

For a moment he looked as if he might dispute that. For the second time she glimpsed a suggestion of hesitation, uncertainty. She was usually the one hovering on the edge of the unspoken word, afraid that the slightest hint of emotional need would bring the whole edifice of her marriage crashing down about her ears.

Outside, in the real world, wearing her Belle Davenport persona, she wasn't like that. She could play that part without thinking.

And at night, in the privacy of her room where, with one

touch, the brittle politeness melted away, his distance dissolving in the heat of a passion that reduced their world to a population of two, it seemed anything was possible.

But afterwards there was no tenderness, no small talk about their day. He was not interested in her world, had no desire to discuss his own concerns with her. Felt no need to sleep with his arms around her, holding her close for comfort, but left her to her early morning alarm call while he, undisturbed, got on with his real life.

It was the role of wife—beyond the basics of the bedroom—that she'd never been able to fully master. But then, with Miranda immovably entrenched in every other aspect of the role, there had never truly been a vacancy for a wife. Only a concubine.

Hard as this was going to be, she knew it could not be as difficult as staying. 'Can we talk, Ivo?'

'Talk?' His frown was barely perceptible, but it was there. 'Now?'

'Yes, now.'

'Don't you want to sort yourself out? Take a shower?' He glanced back at his desk. He didn't have to say the words; it was plain that he had more important things to do.

'For heaven's sake, Ivo, it's Saturday,' she snapped, losing patience, needing to be done with this. Get it over. 'The stock markets are closed.'

'This isn't…' he began. Then, 'It'll take ten minutes, fifteen at the most.'

She'd been away for weeks. Any other man would have dropped whatever he was doing, eager to see her, talk to her, ask how she was, how it had been. Tell her that he was glad to have her home. If he'd done that, she thought, the words sitting like a lump in her throat would have dissolved, evaporated. She could not have said them. But for Ivo business always came first, while she was an inconvenience, a constant reminder of his one weakness…

'Why don't you go up? I'll be there just as soon as I've finished this,' he suggested and, without waiting, he turned back to his desk. 'We can talk then.'

No. That wasn't how it worked. Not that he wouldn't come. Fifteen minutes from now she'd be in the shower and he'd join her there, demonstrating with his body, as he never could with words, exactly how much he'd missed her.

The only thing they wouldn't do was talk.

Afterwards, after the drugging pleasures of his body that would drive everything from her mind, she'd wake, as always alone—he'd have gone back to work—and there would be some trinket left at the bedside: something rare and beautiful, befitting her status as his wife, an acknowledgement that he'd been selfish, unreasonable about the Himalayan trip. She would wear whatever it was at dinner, a wordless acceptance of his unspoken apology.

Not today, she promised herself, her hand tightening around the tiny cellphone in her pocket—a direct connection to Simone, Claire. Women who knew more about her than her own husband. They'd spent every free minute of the last few days talking about their lives, the past, the future; they had listened, understood, cared about her in ways he never could. With them to support her she would find the strength to break out of the compartment he'd made for her. He might be satisfied with this relationship— and why wouldn't he be?—but she needed more, much more...

'No, Ivo.' Already, in his head, back with whatever project she'd interrupted, he didn't seem to hear her. 'I'm afraid it won't.' He stopped, turned slowly. 'Wait.'

His skin was taut across his face, emphasising the high cheek-bones, the aristocratic nose, a mouth that could reduce her to mindless, whimpering jelly and, looking at him, Belle found it achingly hard to say the words that would put an end to her marriage.

He did nothing to help her but, keeping his distance, the tips of his fingers resting on the corner of his desk, a barrier between them, he waited, still and silent, for her to speak. It was almost, she thought, as if he knew what she was going to say. If so, he knew more than she did.

'This is difficult,' she began.

'Then...then my advice is to keep it simple.' His voice,

usually crisp and incisive, was slightly blurred. Or maybe it was him that was blurred behind a veil of something she was very afraid might be tears.

'Yes,' she said, and blinked to clear her vision. No tears. She'd learned a long time ago not to show that kind of weakness. 'Yes,' she said again. This was not something that could be wrapped up in soft words. Somehow made less painful with padding. Simple, direct, to the point, with no possibility of misunderstanding. That was the way to do it. 'I'm sorry but I can't live with you any more, Ivo. I'm setting you free of our deal.'

'Free?'

'We said, didn't we, that it wasn't a till-death-us-do-part deal. That either of us could walk away at any time.' Then, when he did not respond, 'I'm walking away, Ivo.'

Predicting his reaction to such a bald announcement had been beyond her, but if she'd hoped that his cool façade would finally crack, she'd have been disappointed. There was no visible reaction. He looked neither shocked nor surprised, but then he'd made a life's work of being unreadable, keeping the world guessing. The fact that he could do it to her confirmed everything she had known about her marriage, but until last week had been too weak to confront.

His response, when it finally came, was practical rather than emotional. 'Where will you go?'

That was it?

Not, 'Why?' Or did he believe he already knew the answer to that? Assumed that the only reason she would leave him was because she'd found someone else? The thought sickened her....

'Does it matter?' she asked abruptly.

'Yes, it matters...' He bit off the words, shook his head. 'Manda will need to know where to forward your mail.'

On the point of saying something very rude about his sister, she stopped herself. This was not Miranda's fault. And she was not hiding from him, running away. Just distancing herself. For both their sakes. 'The tenants moved out of my flat last month,' she explained. 'I'll stay there.'

'That won't do—'

'It's what I want,' she cut in before he could take over and set about organising accommodation that he considered more acceptable for someone who bore his name.

He didn't look happy about it, but he let it go and said, 'Very well.' Then, 'Is that it?'

No!

Her heart cried out the word, but she kept her mouth closed and, getting no answer, he nodded and returned to his desk to resume the work she had interrupted.

Numb, frozen out, cut off by a wall of ice, she was left with nothing to do but pack her immediate needs and leave.

Miranda emerged from the dining room as she headed for the stairs.

'Belle? What are you doing here? I didn't expect you back until tomorrow.'

'It's lovely to see you too,' she said, without stopping, without looking back.

Ivo Grenville was staring blindly at the document in front of him when his sister, taking advantage of the door that Belle hadn't bothered to close on her way out, walked into the library.

'What's the matter with Belle?' she asked. Then, without waiting for an answer, 'Honestly, she might have had the good manners to let me know she was coming back today.'

'Why should she? This is her…' He faltered on the word 'home', but his sister was too busy waving his objection away with an impatient gesture to notice.

'That's not the point. Even if I can drum up another man for tonight, I'll have to totally rearrange the seating. And the caterers are going to—'

'No.'

'No? You mean she won't be joining us for dinner?' She relaxed. 'Well, thank goodness for that. To be honest, she did look a mess, but I've no doubt people would run around, pull out all the stops for her. One smile and people just fall over themselves—'

'No!' He so rarely raised his voice, and never to her, that she was shocked into silence. 'You won't have to rearrange the seating because tonight's dinner is cancelled.'

'Cancelled?' Her laugh, uncertain, died as she saw his face. 'Ivo…?' Then, 'Don't be ridiculous. I can't cancel this late. The Ambassador, the Foreign Secretary… What possible reason can I give?'

'I neither know nor care, but if you're stuck for an excuse why don't you tell our guests that my wife has just announced that she's leaving me and I'm not in the mood to make small talk. I'm sure they'll understand.'

'Leaving you? But she can't!' Then, flushing, 'Oh, I see. Who—'

'Manda, please,' he said, cutting her off before she could put into words the thoughts that had flashed through his mind. Thoughts that shamed him. Belle had never been less than forthright, honest with him. She'd wanted security; he'd wanted her… 'Not another word.'

He heard the door close very quietly and finally he sat back, abandoning the documents that moments before he'd insisted were too important to wait. Nothing was that important but, in the instant when he'd looked up and seen Belle, he'd known what was coming. It was in her eyes, the look he'd been waiting for, dreading, had always known would one day come. Security, for a woman of such warmth, such passion, was never going to be enough.

His first thought had been to postpone it, delay it, do anything to give himself time.

Another hour. Another day…

Each and every day of his working life he took a few precious minutes out of his morning to watch her as she lit up the television screen in his office. Each day, while she'd been away, he'd seen the change in her, had felt her moving away from him, had recognised the danger. Maybe it had begun even before she'd left; he just hadn't wanted to see it. Maybe that was why he had tried so hard to stop her going on the trip.

He opened the desk drawer, pushing aside the ticket to Hong

Kong, bought on the day he'd watched, agonised, as she'd talked into the camera, smiling even though there was blood trickling down her face. Plans he'd been forced to abandon when a crisis had blown up over a project he'd embarked upon.

He'd told himself that it didn't matter. That he would drive down to the airport and meet her flight. Give her the necklace he'd had made for her with the diamonds his mother had worn on her wedding day.

Wrong on both counts.

Belle didn't bother with the shower; she didn't want to spend one minute more than necessary in this house. What she did need were clothes, and since she was due back at work first thing on Monday morning that involved rather more than a change of underwear and a pair of jeans.

She stared helplessly at the dozens of outfits that had been carefully chosen to provoke the desire in the red-blooded male to wake up each morning to her presence on the television screen, the wish in every female breast to be her best friend.

It was a difficult trick to pull off. Between them, however, the designers and the image consultants had managed it. Everything about her that the public recognised as 'Belle Davenport', her life, her marriage, had been airbrushed so thoroughly that she'd forgotten what was real and what was little more than a media fabrication.

Maybe that was why, for so long, she had felt she was running on empty. That if she stopped concentrating for a second the floor would open up beneath her feet and she'd disappear.

Suddenly losing it, unable to keep up the pretence for another minute, she turned her back on them and tossed the bare essentials in a holdall—underwear, shoes, a few basics, the first things that came to hand.

What else? She looked around. Make-up...

She grabbed for a gold-topped glass pot but her hands were shaking and it slipped through her fingers, shattered, splashing pale beige cream in a wide arc over the centuries-old polished oak floor, an antique rug. With a cry of dismay, she bent to pick up the pieces of glass.

'Leave it!'

Ivo...

'Leave it,' he said, taking her hand, pulling it away from the glass. 'You'll cut yourself.'

Her skin shivered at his touch; his hand was cool and yet heat radiated from his fingers, warming her—as he never failed to warm her—so that the siren call of everything in her that was female urged her to let him lift her up into his arms, to hold him, tell him that she didn't mean it. That she would never leave him. That nothing else mattered but to be here with him.

He touched her cheek, then pushed back her hair to look at the graze on her forehead, regarding her with eyes the colour of the ocean, a shifting mix of blue, green, grey that, as with the sea, betrayed his mood. Today they were a bleak grey, her doing she knew, and she forced herself to turn away from his touch as if to gather up the rest of her make-up. It was easier to cope with his reflection in the mirror than face to face.

'Is this because I didn't want you to go away, Belle?' he asked, his hands on her shoulders, his thumbs working softly against the muscles, easing the tension as they had done times without number in a prelude to an intimacy that needed no words.

His touch shivered through her, undermining her will. She'd lingered too long. He'd taken it as a sign that she was just having a bit of a strop, throwing her teddy out of the pram, was waiting for him to come up and make a performance of appeasing her.

'No,' she said. That he didn't want her to go away was understandable, but she couldn't allow him to use her weakness to stop her from leaving. 'It's because we don't have a marriage, Ivo. We don't share anything. Because I want something you're incapable of giving.'

In the mirror she saw him blench.

'You're my wife, Belle. Everything I have is yours—'

'I'm your weakness, Ivo,' she said, cutting him short. This

wasn't about property, security. 'You desire me. You have a need that I satisfy.'

'And you? Don't I satisfy you?'

'Physically? You know the answer to that.' When he held her, the flames of that desire were enough to warm her, body and soul. But when he turned away she was left with ice. 'You have given me everything that I asked of you. But what we have is not a marriage.'

'You're tired,' he said, his voice cobweb-soft against her ear. The truth was it didn't matter what he said, her response to his undivided attention had always been the same; she was a rabbit fixed in the headlights of an oncoming car, unable to move, save herself and her body responded as it always did, softening to him. He felt the change and, sure of his power, he turned her to face him. Instinct drew her to him and she leaned into the haven of his body, waiting for him to tell her that he'd missed her, to ask her what was wrong, to do what she'd asked and talk to her.

Instead he took something from his pocket. A strand of fire that blazed in the light as he moved to fasten it about her neck.

'I had this made for you for our anniversary next month.'

'It's not our anniversary…'

'The anniversary of the day we first met.'

Belle felt as if she were being split in two. The physical half was standing safe, protected, within the circle of Ivo's arms. But all of her that was emotion, heart, the woman who'd dug deep and, with the help of her friends, found the strength to confront her past, stood outside, looking on with horror as she was drawn in by this glittering proof that he had thought of her, cherished the memory of the moment when their lives had first connected.

'No…'

She barely whispered the word as the gems touched her throat. A single thread of diamonds to circle her neck. Beautiful.

Cold.

If his heart was a diamond, maybe he could have given her that. But the warm, beating flesh required more, something that was beyond him. That she had once thought was beyond her…

'Please, Ivo. Don't do this…'

It took a supreme act of will to force up her chin, look him directly in the face, find the strength to break free, for both of them.

'No,' she repeated, this time with more certainty. And, taking a step back, she brushed the necklace away, taking him by surprise so that it flew from his hand, skidded across the floor.

This wasn't about desire. Not for him. It wasn't even as basic as lust. This was all about control.

'No more.'

She took another step away, then turned and, abandoning her make-up, she picked up her bag, holding him at arm's length when, instinctively, he made a move to take it from her.

Only then, when she was sure he would keep his distance, did she turn, walk away on legs that felt as if they were treading on an underfilled airbed. On feet that didn't seem to be one hundred per cent in contact with the ground.

Every part of her hurt. It was worse than that first day on the mountains when she'd thought she'd die if she had to force her feet to push the pedal one more time.

That had been purely physical pain. Muscle, sinew, bone.

This cut to the heart. If she'd ever doubted how much she loved him, every step taking her away from him hammered the message home. But love, true love, involved sacrifice. Ivo had taken her on trust, had accepted without question everything she'd told him about her life before they'd met. Before she became 'Belle Davenport'. She'd done two utterly selfish things in her life—abandoned her sister and married Ivo Grenville. It was time to confront the past, find the courage to put both of those things right.

Her rucksack was where she'd left it, battered, grubby, out of place in the perfection of the Regency hall. They were a match, she thought, as she picked it up, slung it over her shoulder. She'd always been out of place here. A stranger in her own life.

The door had been propped open by the florists who were ferrying in boxes of flowers. Grateful that she wouldn't have to find the strength to open it, she walked down the steps and out into the street.

On her own again and very much 'scared witless...' but certain, as she hadn't been for a very long time, of the rightness of what she was doing.

Belle's flat—small, slightly shabby—welcomed her as the great house in Belgravia never had. Unable to believe her good fortune, she'd bought it the moment she'd signed her first contract following one of those chance-in-a-million breaks. Her fairy-godmother had come in the unlikely guise of a breakfast show host who, when her brief appearance manning the phones on the telethon he was presenting had lit up the switchboard, had run with it and, playing up to the public's response, had offered her a guest appearance on his show. Not quite knowing what to do with her, he'd suggested she do a weather spot.

For some reason her flustered embarrassment at her very shaky grasp of geography had touched the viewers' hearts.

One of the gossip magazines had run a feature on her and within weeks she'd had an agent and a serious contract to go out and talk to people in the street, in their offices, in their homes, asking their opinions on anything from the price of bread to the latest health fad.

Even now she didn't understand how it had happened but, from a situation where she and her bank did their best to ignore each other, suddenly she was being invited into the manager's office for a chat over a cup of coffee. They hadn't been able to do enough for her, especially once she'd demonstrated that investing in bricks and mortar—securing herself a home against the time when the sympathy wore thin—had been her first priority.

Against all the odds, she'd gradually moved from her spot as light relief to the centre of the breakfast television sofa, picking up the long-term security of a multi-millionaire husband on the way.

But she'd kept her flat.

She hadn't needed Ivo—financial genius that he was—to advise her to let it rather than sell it when they'd married. She would never part with it. It wasn't just that it was a good investment, that it had been her first, her only proper home; it represented, at some fundamental level, a different, truthful kind of security.

After her last tenant had left she'd made the excuse that it needed refurbishing and taken it off the agency books. Almost as if she'd been preparing for this moment.

Shivering, she dumped her bags in the hall, switched on the heating. Looked around. Touched one of the walls for reassurance. The stones in her wedding ring caught the light, flashed back at her, and she stood there for a moment, lost in the memory of the moment when Ivo had placed it on her finger. Then it had been the sun that had caught the stones in the antique ring as he'd pledged to keep her safe, protect her.

He had. He'd done everything he'd promised. But it wasn't enough. And she slipped the ring from her finger.

Then, in a frenzy of activity, she made the bed, unpacked her things. Stuffed everything into the washing machine.

Ivo was wrong. She wasn't tired. Her body clock was all over the place and she was buzzing. Once she'd showered, she sorted herself out a pair of trousers, a shirt, a sweater from the jumbled mess in her bag, made a cup of tea and switched on her computer.

Her first priority was to send emails to Claire and Simone to let them know that she was home safely. Update them.

…I've moved into my old flat. It needs redecorating, but that's okay. It'll be something to keep me busy in the long winter evenings.

She added a little wry smiley.

I hope you both had uneventful trips home since I suspect life is about to get a little bumpy for all of us. Take care. Love, Belle.

She hit 'send'. Sat back. Remembered Simone's face as she'd warned her against doing anything hasty. Telling her that Ivo could help…

No. This was something she had to do herself. And, brushing

aside the ache, she began to search the 'net for information on how she could find her sister.

The good news was that new legislation meant that not only mothers could register to contact children given up for adoption, but family too.

The bad news was that Daisy had to make the first move.

Unless she'd signed up to find her birth family—and, for the life of her, Belle couldn't imagine why she would want to—there would be no connection.

Ivo could help…

The tempting little voice whispered in her ear. He would have contacts…

She shut it out, filled in the online form with all the details she had. If that produced no results, there were agencies that specialised in helping to trace adopted family members.

She'd give it a week before she went down that route. Right now, she had a more pressing concern. She had to call her hairdresser and grovel.

'Eeuw…' George, her stylist, a man who understood a hair emergency when he saw it, picked up a dry blonde strand to examine its split ends and shuddered. 'I knew it was going to be bad but really, Belle, this is shocking. What have you being doing to it?'

'Nothing.'

'I suppose that would explain it. I hope you haven't got any plans for the rest of the day. It's going to need a conditioning treatment, colour—'

'I want you to cut it,' Belle said, before he could get into his stride.

'Well, obviously. These ends will have to go.'

'No. Cut it. Short. And let's lose the platinum blonde, um? Go for something nearer my real colour.'

'Oh, right. And can you remember what that is?' he asked, arching a brow at her in the mirror.

Vaguely. She'd started off white blonde, like her sister, but her own hair had darkened as she'd got older. She'd reversed the process as soon as she'd discovered the hair colouring aisle in the supermarket, but if she was going for 'real', her hair was as good a place as any to start.

'Cheerful mouse?' she offered.

'An interesting concept, darling. Somehow I don't think it will catch on.' Then, having examined her roots, presumably to check for himself, he said, 'Have you cleared this with your image consultant? Your agent?' When she didn't respond, 'Your husband?'

The mention of Ivo brought a lump to her throat.

She fought it down.

It was her hair, her image, her life and, by way of answer, she leaned forward, picked up a pair of scissors lying on the ledge in front of her, extended a lock of hair and, before George could stop her, she cut through it, just below her ear. Then, still holding the scissors, she said, 'Do you want to finish it or shall I?'

CHAPTER THREE

SHOPPING was not Belle's usual method of displacement activity, but when she'd finally woken on Sunday the reality of what she'd done, of being alone—not just alone in her bed but alone for ever—had suddenly hit home and the day seemed to stretch like a desert ahead of her.

Finding herself sitting at her computer, waiting for an email with news of Daisy, leaping on an incoming message, only to discover it was some unspeakably vile spam, she forced herself to move.

She didn't know how the Adoption Register worked, but it was the weekend and it seemed unlikely she'd hear from anyone before the middle of the week at the earliest. More likely the middle of next month.

For the moment there was nothing more she could do and, besides, she had a much more immediate problem. She had nothing to wear for work on Monday.

Clearly, she rationalized, the sensible thing would be to call Ivo and arrange to go and pick up at least part of her wardrobe. She had a new pale pink suit that would show off her tan, look great with her new hair colouring. And she had to have shoes. There were a hundred things...

Or maybe just one.

Last night she'd felt so utterly alone. She had yearned for that brief flare of passion in Ivo's eyes. To know that there was one person in the world who needed her, if only for a moment.

Pathetic.

But if she went back today, if he launched another attack on her senses when she was at her lowest, she suspected she would not be strong enough to resist. And what then?

If, by some miracle, she found Daisy, she would be torn in two. She would have to deny Daisy a second time or tell him everything. Tell him that, far from being up front and honest with him, she had lied and lied and lied. That he didn't know the woman he'd married.

And she'd lose him all over again.

At least this way she retained some dignity, the possibility that if, when, the truth came out, he would—maybe—understand. Be grateful for the distance. Even be happy for her.

Which was all very well and noble, but it still left her with the problem of what she was going to wear tomorrow.

Since she needed to get out of the flat before she succumbed to temptation, she dealt with both problems in one stroke and called a taxi—no more chauffeur on tap—and took herself off to one of the vast shopping outlets that had sprung up around London and lost herself among the crowds.

She had been told often enough that the golden rule was to change your hair or change your clothes but not both at the same time. As she flipped through the racks of clothes, she ignored it. She was done with living by other people's rules.

She fell in love with an eau-de-nil semi-tailored jacket. Exactly the kind of thing her style 'guru' had warned her not to wear. She wasn't tall enough or thin enough to carry it off, apparently. On the contrary, she barely made five and a half feet and her figure was of the old-fashioned hourglass shape. But all that cycling had at least had one good outcome—she was trimmer all over. And with her hair cut short she felt taller.

She lifted the collar, pushed up the sleeves and was rewarded with a smile from the saleswoman.

'That looks great on you.' Then, 'Did anyone ever tell you that you look a lot like Belle Davenport?'

'No,' she said truthfully. Then, 'She wouldn't wear something like this, would she?'

'No, but you're thinner than her. And taller.'

Belle grinned. 'You think so? They do say that television adds ten pounds.'

'Trust me, you look fabulous.'

She felt fabulous, but she was so accustomed to listening to advice that she had little confidence in her own judgement. But the other jackets—neat, waist-hugging 'Belle Davenport' style jackets in pastel colours—that she'd tried were more expensive, so the woman had no incentive to lie.

'Thank you,' she said. And bought its twin in a fine brown tweedy mixture that looked perfect with her new hair and matched her eyes. Then she set about teaming them with soft cowl necks, classic silk shirts, trousers—she always wore skirts on air—and neat ankle boots.

More than once, as she browsed through the racks, she saw someone take a second glance, but her new haircut and George's brilliant streaky blend of light brown through to sun-kissed blonde—his very inventive interpretation of cheerful mouse—fooled them. She couldn't possibly be who they thought she was.

There was an exhilarating freedom in this moment of anonymity and when she spotted a photo booth she piled in with her packages, grinning into the camera as she posed for a picture so that she could share the joke with Claire and Simone.

Then she passed an interior design shop.

She wasn't the only one that needed a make-over and if time was going to be hanging heavy on her hands she might as well make a start on the flat.

When she was done there, she was so laden with the in-house designer's print outs, swatches, carpet squares and colour charts that she had to call it a day and take another taxi. At which point she wondered about buying herself a car.

One of her very early 'make a fool of Belle' projects for the television had been a driving course. Not that much of a fool, actually, since she'd taken to it like a duck to water and ended up doing an off-road course, a circuit in a grand prix car and driving a double-decker bus through a skid test. And earned herself another contract.

She'd bought a little car then, but once she'd married Ivo there had always been a chauffeur in town and there had been no point in keeping it.

The taxi driver was a mine of information on the subject and by the time he delivered her to her door he'd made a call arranging for her to test drive a zippy little BMW convertible the following afternoon.

'You did what?'

She hadn't long been home from the studio on Monday afternoon when the doorbell rang.

Her first thought was that it was the press who, following up her appearance on the television that morning, would be clamouring for the story behind her 'new look'. Since neither her agent nor her PR consultant could answer their questions— she hadn't talked to either of them yet—the gossip columnists would have called the house, which meant they would now have a much bigger story.

That she was no longer living with Ivo. That the 'perfect' marriage was over.

Of course it could be her agent—he kept a television on in his office so that he could keep an eye on his clients—demanding to know what on earth she thought she was doing, messing with success. Ruining the image he'd gone to so much trouble and expense—he always took expenditure personally, even when it was her money he was spending—to build. Anxious to arrange interviews, a photo session so that he could 'sell' her new look. Wanting to know what spin the PR guys should put on the fact that she'd moved out of the family home, since, like the press, he'd go there first.

A new romance for her? *Positive, upbeat, radiant…*

A cheating husband? *Sympathetic, brave…*

A marriage that had collapsed under the strain of the pressure of their careers? *Very sad. Still good friends…*

She'd seen it all a hundred times.

The light on the answering machine had been flashing when

she'd got home. She had ignored it, just as she now ignored the doorbell.

Instead, she was glued to her laptop, anxiously checking through the messages to see if there was anything from the Adoption Register.

Nothing. Instead she clicked on the site she'd bookmarked, the one with personal adoption stories.

A second longer peal on the bell warned her that whoever was at the front door wasn't about to go away and, knowing that she would have to face the music sooner rather than later, she picked up the entry phone.

'Yes?' she said, her voice neutral.

'Belle…'

She caught her breath, almost doubling up with shock at the sound of Ivo's voice…

No…

It was the middle of the afternoon. He should be in his office, all of London at his feet, both figuratively and metaphorically. He didn't do 'personal', not in office hours. Not ever…

She didn't answer, couldn't answer, just buzzed him up, taking the time it took for him to walk up to her flat—an old converted town house, there were no lifts—to recover. Taking those few moments to put herself back together before she opened the door.

For a moment he just looked at her.

Then he reached out, as if he needed to touch the short flicked up layers of her hair before he could bring himself to believe what she'd done. Curled his long fingers back into his palm before he made contact.

'You look…'

Words apparently failed him. That was twice in three days. If she wasn't struggling for words herself, she might have derived a certain amount of satisfaction from that.

'Different?' she managed, when it seemed that nothing would break the silence.

He shook his head, but offered no alternative, just lifted the thick wad of envelopes he was holding as if that was enough to explain his presence.

For a minute there her heart, not quite keeping up with her head, had hoped for something more. What, quite, she didn't know, but something. Doing her best to ignore its dizzy spin—she'd had a lifetime of hiding her thoughts, her feelings; three years of marriage to practise hiding them from Ivo: it shouldn't be this hard—she said, 'I thought Miranda was going to forward my post.'

'It's piled up while you were away. Some of it might be important.'

So important that he'd left his office early to bring it to her, rather than send a messenger? *Was* there anything that important?

She held out her hand to take the bundle of envelopes, but he didn't surrender it.

'I called earlier.'

Twice? He'd come twice...

'I have a letterbox,' she said. 'You could have left it.'

'It wasn't just the mail.' No. As she'd suspected, his presence on her doorstep had nothing to do with her post. 'You're usually home long before this.'

'Today wasn't usual. I've been away and there was a lot to catch up with. And I had a couple of meetings that ran on.' A bit of an understatement. Having done the hard one—telling Ivo that she was leaving him—her calm announcement that she wouldn't be renewing her contract to anchor the breakfast television show had been a piece of cake.

And yet here she was making excuses like some kid justifying herself for being late home from school. Not that she ever had been. School had been a dangerous luxury, something she'd had to steal...

It was time to remind Ivo, as well as herself, that she had to make excuses to no one.

'And then I bought a car,' she added, as casually as if she was telling him she'd bought a new pair of shoes.

Which was when her very cool and detached husband became distinctly heated.

'You did what?'

Not so much a question as a man displaying outrage that a woman—his wife, no less—had the audacity to believe herself capable of making that kind of decision for herself.

It had, actually, been quite a week for decisions:

Left her husband.

Had her hair cut.

Bought a car.

So far, it was the car that had got the biggest reaction so she stayed with that.

'It's a BMW convertible,' she told him. 'Silver. Only twenty-two thousand miles on the clock. It's being delivered tomorrow.'

'It's not new?' First outrage, now concern. 'Has it been checked? Please tell me it's not a private sale.'

Extraordinary. If she'd realised it would get this kind of response she'd have bought a car before. Several of them. Maybe gone into the used car business...

'Would that be bad?'

'I'll need the registration number so that I can run a check. It could be stolen. Or a couple of stitched together wrecks. And the mileage is undoubtedly fake. Have you any idea—'

'Oh, no,' she assured him. If he was going to treat her like a dumb blonde, then—hair colour notwithstanding—she'd had plenty of practice playing the role. 'I'm sure it's fine. I bought it from the brother-in-law of a taxi driver I met yesterday.'

He didn't actually groan, but he didn't look impressed. He wasn't meant to.

'Give me his name and address.'

'The taxi driver?'

'His brother-in-law,' Ivo said, not quite through gritted teeth, but she could see that it was a close call.

It served him right for acting as if she was too stupid to live, she thought. If he'd watched her show once in a while he would have known that they had, on more than one occasion, run features on all aspects of buying used cars.

'Oh, Mike!' she said, determined to rub it in. 'Such a sweet man. Hold on, I've got his card somewhere.' Her bag was lying on the hall table and she opened it, produced a business card, offered it to him.

Ivo took it, looked at it, then at her. 'Mike Wade is the taxi driver's brother-in-law?'

'Yes.' Then, 'Is there something wrong?' Beyond the fact that, too late, he'd realised she'd been winding him up since Mike Wade was a senior representative at one of London's premier BMW dealerships rather than some dodgy character selling used cars off the street.

'He asked to be remembered to you,' she added. 'Said you'd been in to talk about exchanging your car for one of the smaller models. Very green...'

Then, exhilarating as it should have been to discover that Ivo was not made of stone, that it was possible to wind him up, she found herself regretting it. He was just looking out for her. Making sure that she was okay.

Actually, she was doing fine and he had to understand that so, dropping the teasing, refusing to hope that the thought that she might be with someone else had been gnawing away at him all weekend, until he'd been driven to come and find out for himself, she said, 'Why are you here, Ivo?'

'I wondered what you wanted to do about your clothes,' he said, returning the card, then running his fingers distractedly through a lick of hair that had the temerity to slide across his forehead. 'There must be things you'll need.'

'Yes.'

The word came out on a sigh that she was unable to quite stifle.

Not uncontrollable jealousy, then, just the practicalities. And of course, infuriatingly, he was right. It took more than a day of self-indulgence to replace an entire wardrobe. A few jackets and shirts wouldn't take her far. Apart from anything else, she had a television awards dinner coming up.

She'd already bought an antique Balenciaga gown for the occasion. It would be her first public appearance without Ivo and if the clothes were eye-catching enough, maybe people wouldn't remark on his absence. Maybe she wouldn't notice it too much.

'And we need to talk,' he added. 'About what happens next.'

'You'd better come through,' she said, turning away, leaving him to follow. Then, because facing him in her small sitting room while he coldly deconstructed their lives was unbearable, she veered off into the kitchen and once there needed to do something with her hands. 'Are you hungry?' she asked. 'It seems forever since lunch.' A sandwich at a hastily convened meeting in the boardroom. Not that she'd eaten any of it. One mouthful had warned her that it would stick like a lump of glue in her throat. Then, when he didn't immediately answer, she turned and realised he hadn't followed. She retraced her steps and found him staring at her laptop. The adoption site.

'You're busy,' he said. 'I've disturbed you.'

He'd disturbed her the moment she'd turned and seen him looking at her at some charity function. When she'd felt the heat reach out and touch her from the far side of the room.

It had been new then, but the effect did not diminish with familiarity; even now it seemed to burn through her silk shirt, warming her skin.

'I'm researching a new project,' she said, her fingers itching to close the lid, but her brain warning her that hiding what she was doing would only arouse his interest. Then, 'I haven't got much in. Food,' she added. Just the basics she'd picked up at the eight-'til-late on the corner.

The computer beeped to warn her of an incoming email and the sound seemed to vibrate through her. *Daisy...*

It took every bit of will-power she possessed to turn away and walk into the kitchen.

'It'll have to be something on toast,' she said. 'Cheese? Sardines?' The kind of comfort food that had no place in his Belgravia kitchen, but which she craved right now. 'Scrambled eggs—'

'We could go somewhere.' Clearly he felt as out of place in her kitchen as—all Savile Row tailoring and handmade shirts—he looked.

'I don't think so.'

'Somewhere quiet,' he persisted, unused to his suggestions meeting with resistance.

She didn't argue, just took a box of eggs from the fridge. 'You'll find some bread in the crock,' she said, as she set about cracking them, one by one into a bowl.

For a moment he didn't move, then, dropping the envelopes on the counter, he reached for the loaf.

'You didn't know I could cook, did you?' she said, reaching up to unhook a whisk, doing her best to keep it light.

'You've never needed to,' he said as he put the loaf down beside her.

Not since she'd married him.

She'd watched the television chefs who'd been on her show. Had bought books, taught herself. It had been such a luxury to have her own kitchen. Such a pleasure to be able to go to the supermarket and buy what she wanted. But in Ivo's house there had always been someone on hand to produce anything from a sandwich to a banquet at the drop of a hat and her early visits to the kitchen had been firmly discouraged by Miranda on the grounds that it would upset the staff.

'Maybe I did,' she said.

When he didn't answer, she looked up, realised just how close he was. How foolish she'd been to invite him in. She needed to keep her distance…

'Why don't you make the toast?' she suggested, moving away to pour egg into a pan. Scrambling eggs was not rocket science, but it did require total concentration, which was why she'd made that the comfort food of choice. 'You *do* know how to make toast?'

'I went to a spartan, character-building public school in the wilds of Scotland,' he reminded her. 'Followed by four years at university, Belle. Without a toaster I'd have starved.'

His words, about twice as much as he'd ever said before about his school days, were unexpectedly heartfelt. He didn't talk much about his childhood. All she knew she'd learned from Miranda. Their summers in France and Italy, the ponies, the pets…

Now she wondered. Had he been as happy as Manda had implied?

'There's a difference between being hungry and starving,' she said, refusing to weaken, look at him. Besides, she wasn't talking about food.

She'd only ever envied Ivo one thing. Not his wealth, a house filled with treasures gathered over generations, the half a dozen places around the world he could call home if ever he had the time to visit them. Only his education. The fact that he and Miranda had conversations about art, music, literature that passed right over her head. That, courtesy of summers spent in France and Italy all through their apparently idyllic childhood, they spoke both languages fluently.

She'd missed out on so much, had spent all her adult life reading voraciously in an attempt to fill the gaps, but mostly learned just how much she didn't know.

He'd had every advantage. Had no business complaining.

'My staff sponsored you,' he said, assuming that she was referring to the kids they'd been raising money to help. 'Supported what you were doing.'

'Am I supposed to be grateful?' she asked, unimpressed, as she continued to stir the egg. 'They were just sucking up to the boss, Ivo.'

'You underestimate yourself.' Then, when she was surprised into looking at him, 'They were genuinely touched by your empathy with those children.'

'Oh.' Throat suddenly dry, she said, 'And you?'

'I supported you too. A cheque was sent into your appeal this morning from all of us.'

'Thank you,' she said, knowing that it would be generous, wishing she hadn't been quite so sharp. 'But I was asking if you were "genuinely touched".'

'Belle…'

Stupid question…

The bread popped up and, glad of the interruption, she took the eggs from the heat, reached for plates from the overhead rack. 'Will you pass me the butter from the fridge?'

He didn't move. 'What is this all about? Why now?' When she didn't answer, he added, 'If there's no one else?'

The painful edge of uncertainty in his voice was so rare, so unexpected, that she had to put down the wooden spoon she'd been using to stir the eggs. The one thing about Ivo that was unchanging was his sureness of purpose and she longed to go to him, to reassure him that this was not his fault.

Unfortunately there was only one way that would end, so instead she fetched the butter herself, spread it on the toast, piled on the egg and hitched herself up on a stool with the breakfast bar between them. Only then could she trust herself to say, 'There's no one else, Ivo.'

She picked up a fork, going through the motions of normality for both of them.

'As for why now—well, maybe distance lends perspective.' She toyed with the egg, searching for words that would explain how she felt without unnecessarily hurting him. 'We never pretended that this was a fairy tale marriage, Ivo, and we've had three years.' She managed a wry smile. 'That's at least two years longer than most people gave us at the start. Almost a record for someone in my business. At least we knew what the score was. Didn't make the mistake of having children...' Her voice faltered and she gripped the fork more tightly, as if it were a lifeline. 'There's no one to be hurt.'

Grateful...

Now that really was a fairy tale.

She'd longed for Ivo's baby, a part of him who would love her unreservedly, accept her as she was, but she had married him for security, he'd married her for lust. Children needed more than that.

Maybe 'grateful' was the right word.

Babies would have been no more than a sticking plaster to cover over the hollow place in her life. The Daisy-shaped emptiness that, until now, she'd refused to acknowledge.

Until she'd confronted the past, found her sister, she had no right to children of her own.

'Just accept that I'm doing us both a favour,' she said, a little desperately. 'Let it go. Find someone who'll fit your world…'

Grateful.

The small kitchen seemed to darken and Ivo felt something inside him contract.

Belle had always been too big to squeeze into the narrow confines of his cold world. She had always been brighter, warmer, more alive. A place where he could lose himself, forget who he was for a while. When he was with her, he was the best he could be but she deserved more and had, apparently, finally realised that.

It was as if, out there in the high mountains, she had reached into herself, had found the confidence to abandon a perfectly honed image that the public adored, replacing it with a new, more powerful, maturer look to take her into a new decade. As if she'd somehow tapped into an inner strength that made her at once more desirable, less attainable.

She no longer needed a prop. No longer needed him.

Once, all he would have had to do was reach out, touch her and she would have been his but his attempt to stop her from leaving had, in its desperation, been so clumsy that she'd rejected him out of hand.

To bring her back now, to hold on to her, would be selfish beyond belief. And yet he could not let her go. And did not know how to keep her.

If she were a company he'd know what to do. He could interpret the balance sheets, analyse performance, formulate a plan…

'Someone who will give you what I never could,' she finished.

'You give me—'

The words began to spill out before Ivo could stop them.

'I know what I give you,' Belle said, cutting him off before he made a total fool of himself.

The world might think them lost in love, but the world knew nothing.

'I'm sorry,' he said abruptly, indicating the food she'd made him, an ache as familiar as breathing in his throat. To stay and eat with her in such intimacy, such closeness, was a sweetness, an indulgence he would not, could not permit himself. 'I'll have to leave this. I have a meeting.'

Meetings. Mergers. Takeovers. More money. More power. Anything to fill the aching void within him.

Then, unable to just walk away, 'Is there anything you need? Anything I can do for you?'

That was almost a plea, he realised with a jolt and for a moment he thought he might have got to her, but she shook her head.

Finding it harder to leave than he would have believed possible, he looked around the small, hard-used apartment. 'You can't stay here. Give me a day or two and I'll arrange for somewhere more comfortable for you to live.'

'Is that what's worrying you?' she demanded, taking him by surprise as she flared up at him. 'That it won't look good if the world discovers that I'm holed up in a tiny flat near Camden Lock rather than expensively housed in a penthouse in Chelsea Harbour?'

'This isn't about me.' Except that it was. He needed to rid himself of this feeling of helplessness. If he could do something, regain some measure of control...'I just want you to be comfortable. To be safe.' *To come home.* 'This is a very mixed neighbourhood.'

'I know you mean well, Ivo—'

Was a man ever damned with fainter praise?

'—but I need to be in my own place right now.' Then, before he could argue, 'I'll call Miranda and make arrangements to have my things moved from your house.'

Your house...

Not *our* house. Not even the more neutral *the* house, but a place that had been furnished over the centuries, decorated to match its historic importance. More like a museum than somewhere offering the comfort of home.

Somehow they got through the awkwardness of goodbye without touching, using the meaningless words that people say when they don't know what to say.

'If you need anything...'

'I'll call.'

He nodded. 'I'll see myself out,' he said as she made to follow him to the door, not able to face that moment at the door when to kiss her would be unacceptable, not to kiss her would be impossible.

And while he was still strong enough to resist the tug of some force that seemed to draw him inexorably towards her, just as a current drew a drifting ship on to rocks, he walked away, out of her flat, down the steps and out into the busy streets.

His chauffeur opened the door of the Rolls, ready to whisk him back to his ivory tower, but, on the point of stepping in, he changed his mind. Stood back.

'Call the office, let my secretary know that I won't be back today, Paul.'

The man cleared his throat. 'She rang a few minutes ago, Mr Grenville. Threadneedle Street called to ask where you were.'

He had a meeting at the Bank of England and he'd forgotten. Something that had never happened to him before.

'Ask her to call and make my apologies, will you?' Then, 'I won't need you until the morning.' And, without waiting for a reply, he began to walk.

If Belle were a company that he wanted to acquire he'd know what to do.

Look at the balance sheets. Analyse performance. Formulate a plan...

CHAPTER FOUR

BELLE forced herself to eat. She had not been hungry. Cooking had been no more than a distraction, a focus for her eyes, something safe to do with her hands, but the horror of wasting food was too deeply ingrained to simply tip it into the bin and so she chewed food she could not taste, swallowing down a throat choked with pain.

Just because she knew what she was doing was right—right for her and right for Ivo—didn't mean it was easy.

Even now his presence filled the small kitchen, marking her space, owning it with a faint trace of something that lingered in the air. The warmth of his skin, the clean scent of perfectly laundered clothes, something that she couldn't name, but which left her weak with longing, hanging on to the edge of the worktop as if it were a lifeline.

In desperation she grabbed an air freshener from the cupboard beneath the sink and sprayed it around. What had been proved to eradicate the odour of sweaty socks, however, had no discernible effect on the subtler, pervasive essence of Ivo Grenville.

The scent, she realised, was in her head; she would have to live with it until it wore away under the attrition of everyday life. Fading like a bittersweet memory. Or a photograph left in the light.

On autopilot, she forced herself through the motions, rinsing the dishes, putting them in the dishwasher. She wiped down the work surfaces, counting to a hundred before she allowed herself to go to the computer and check the email. Appeasing the Fates with patience, so that the news was more likely to be good. Or maybe just afraid that it wasn't the one she was waiting for.

The Fates clearly thought she needed a little more time.

It was not news about Daisy but an email from Simone, who was in a bit of a flap about losing the diary she'd been writing all through her trip. Confessing that towards the end it had become more an emotional than physical record of her journey, containing the secrets that had spilled out in the clear quiet of the mountains.

If anyone had found it they all risked exposure.

Maybe it was disappointment, or that she was still aching from the encounter with Ivo, but she couldn't bring herself to get worked up about it. But Simone was anxious, full of remorse, and Belle responded with reassurance—the diary was undoubtedly in some airport trash compactor and on the way to landfill by now. Then, because the contact restored her, renewed her conviction in the rightness of what she was doing, she scanned one of the pictures from the strip she'd taken in the photo booth, adding:

I'm attaching a picture of the 'new' me. As you can see, I'm now a little less Monroe, rather more, well, me, I suppose. And not before time. I spent the weekend shopping for new clothes too and not an image consultant in sight. The combination had a blissfully jaw-dropping effect when I walked into the studio at the crack of dawn this morning, an effect that was considerably enhanced when I announced that I wouldn't be renewing my contract.

Ivo dropped by and nearly had a conniption when I told him I'd bought a car...

On the point of telling them about how she'd teased him, she stopped herself. She'd told Claire and Simone that they were separated. To use them to talk about him would be self-indulgence of the worst kind. She had to excise him from her thoughts.

Difficult. Maybe impossible. But she could excise him from her emails... She continued:

But that's just the cosmetic stuff.

My big news is that I've registered with the Adoption Register. If Daisy has done the same, I should be in contact very quickly. If not...

If not, tracking her down could take weeks, months, years... Simone had urged her to ask Ivo for help.

She glanced automatically towards the door, as if half expecting to see him still there, waiting for an answer to his question.

'If you need *anything*...?'

A million things. Help her find Daisy. With his contacts he could probably do it in a second. But truly there was only one thing she wanted from him. His love. But that had never been on offer.

Turning back to the email, she deleted, *If not...*

She would not, must not, allow herself to be sucked in by negative thoughts. Or transmit them to Claire and Simone, who had their own demons to face. Instead she asked how their own plans were going, prompting Claire, in whom she sensed hesitation, not to delay her own search, before signing off, with love.

Then she returned to the adoption website, obsessively reading the stories of people who had been adopted with both wonderful and tragic results. Mothers who had parted with their children. Children hunting for their roots. Stories full of loss, joy, experiences that covered the entire spectrum of emotion. Looking for something that would give her hope, using it to stuff her mind against thoughts of Ivo that, no matter how hard she tried to block them, would seep in and fill her head.

Ivo, on the day they'd stood on a tropical beach, her hand in his as she'd repeated their not to be taken too literally till-death-us-do-part vows. Maybe her heart had known then what her brain had refused to admit.

Ivo, turning away from some close discussion about a major business deal to seek her out, find her at the far end of the dinner table.

Ivo, in a rare moment when he'd fallen asleep in her arms and was, for a brief, blissful moment, entirely hers.

It was late when Ivo finally got home.

'Your secretary rang,' Manda said, her irritation driven, he knew, by anxiety. 'You missed a meeting.'

'I know. I sent my apologies.'

'That's not the point! No one knew where you were.'

'Will I get detention?' he asked.

'Ivo…'

Belle would have laughed. She might have been angry with him, but she wouldn't have been able to help herself. He'd tried so hard not to take more than she had signed up for—the sex and security deal—but she'd drained the tension from him with a smile, a touch.

'You've been to see her, haven't you?' Adding, 'Belle.' As if she could have meant anyone else.

'There were things we needed to talk about.'

Not that they had. Talked. At least not about anything that mattered. But it had been informative, nonetheless. Belle hadn't wanted him looking at her laptop. Had twitched to close it. Hide what she was doing. And she had positively jumped when an email had dropped into her inbox. She was hiding something— not another man, she wouldn't have been able to hide that. Wouldn't have tried to.

He wished he'd taken more notice of what had been on the screen…

'Ivo?'

He realised that his sister was waiting, expecting more, but he shook his head. 'Belle will be in touch about picking up her things.'

'Oh, right, and I'm supposed to snap to attention, I suppose, and run around organising one of the staff to help her pack. Sort out transport to shift it all.'

'I thought you'd relish the moment. Isn't it what you've been waiting for?'

'I… I always knew this would happen.'

'Yes, well, I'm sure you weren't alone.'

'Ivo…'

He turned away from her sympathy, cutting in sharply with, 'If Belle chooses to call ahead as a matter of courtesy it's because she has the instincts of a lady, even if she didn't have the benefit of the most expensive education money can buy.' Then, 'She is my wife, Manda. This is her home.'

'So where is she, hmm?' She made a single sweeping gesture to indicate her absence. As if he needed reminding. 'What is it about her?' she demanded. 'How does she do it? Reduce everyone to drooling mush. She floats about on a cloud of sweetness and light doing absolutely nothing except look glamorous and yet she has the entire world at her feet.'

'If that's all you see, Miranda, then you're not nearly as clever as you think you are,' he said, too angry to use her childhood name.

'Even now, when she's walked out on you, you're defending her.'

'She doesn't need me to defend her.'

Didn't need him for anything. Was that what she'd learned on the mountains? That she was strong enough to stand alone?

'As for the sweetness and light thing,' he added, 'you could, with benefit, try it yourself once in a while.'

His sister flamed, then shrugged, an oddly awkward gesture. 'It's not my style, Ivo.' She lifted her hands in an out of character gesture of helplessness. 'I can't…' Then, 'She makes me feel so…inadequate. As a woman,' she added quickly, in case he thought she meant in any way that was really important. 'The minute she walks into a room I feel as if I've suddenly become invisible…'

'Manda…'

She shook off the moment of weakness, straightened. 'I'll do whatever I can to help,' she said, making an effort to be helpful, 'but wouldn't it be more sensible for Belle to wait until she's moved before collecting more than her basic needs?'

'Moved?'

'You're not going to let her stay in that poky little flat in Camden?'

'I don't appear to have a say in the matter.'

'Oh, I see. She's going to stay put and play poverty to jack up the settlement she'll wring out of you.'

He sighed. That hadn't lasted long.

'Belle will have trouble pleading poverty,' he pointed out. The one thing he had been able to do for her was ensure that her considerable earnings had been well-managed. Maybe that had been his mistake. If her investments had been bungled she would still need the security she craved. That he could offer. 'Wringing will not be necessary, however. Everything I have is hers for the asking.'

'Including this house?'

Unlikely. The one possession of his that Belle would not want, he suspected, would be this house. But he wasn't feeling kind. 'Maybe you'd better start house-hunting yourself,' he advised. 'Just in case. I'm told Camden is going up in the world. Maybe Belle will do a swap. Her flat isn't that poky.'

Not poky at all. It was small in comparison with this house—anything would be small in comparison with it—and shabby, but it had a welcoming warmth which, despite every imaginable luxury, was totally absent from the pile of masonry he called home whenever Belle was absent. And of course that was the point. It was Belle who made the difference.

'Once it's redecorated,' he added, recalling the colour cards and fabric swatches he'd seen lying on the table beside her laptop…

Adoption.

It had been a website about adoption. And suddenly everything fell into place.

'…it'll be fine,' he finished.

The email she'd been waiting for came the next day. Daisy Porter had registered with the agency and had been informed that a family member was looking for her. If she wanted to send a letter they would forward it…

Belle wrote a dozen letters. Long. Short. Every length in between. Finally she summoned a courier—she couldn't wait an extra day for the post—and sent one that contained the bare essentials. No excuses. No apologies. Asking her to write or ring. Giving her address. Her phone number. Her mobile phone number. And, at the last moment, she clipped one of the photographs from the strip she had taken at the photo booth and enclosed that too.

And, because the waiting was unbearable, because she had to do something, she stripped the wallpaper from the living room walls.

By the weekend she wasn't stripping the walls, she was climbing them, so she bought a stepladder and started painting the ceiling. She was working on a fiddly bit of the cornice that decorated her high ceiling when the phone rang, shatteringly loud in a room stripped of curtains and carpet.

She grabbed the handle at the top of the ladder and steadied herself.

She'd expected an instant response from Daisy but, after days of rushing to answer every call, she forced herself to ignore it. Racing up and down a stepladder was just asking for trouble.

It was more likely to be someone from the media who'd finally tracked her down, she told herself, still doing her best to appease the Fates.

So far the studio had managed to keep a lid on the fact that she wasn't renewing her contract. That two weeks from now—unless they could persuade her to change her mind—there would be a new face to go with the cornflakes. And the newspapers and gossip magazines, totally obsessed with her new look—her face ached with smiling at photo sessions—had somehow missed the really big story, that she'd moved out of the marital home. That the smile was not the real thing, but something she had to coax her muscles to do. That it had taken all the make-up artist's skill to cover the dark hollows under her eyes. That her mascara had to be waterproof.

It couldn't last and when the story broke the phone would be her enemy, not her friend.

She should have just given Daisy her cellphone number. Bought a special phone with a number that only she would know. Too late...

The machine picked up, the message played. She'd left the pre-recorded response until she'd heard that Daisy had registered to look for her. Once she'd given her the number, she'd recorded a message in her own voice. Probably a mistake. If it was some gossip columnist hoping to confirm a suspicion, he'd just done it.

She glanced out of the curtainless window, but there were no photographers with long lenses pointed in her direction. No, well—easing her aching shoulder while the message played, hoping against hope that it would be the one call she was waiting for—she still didn't really believe it herself.

The caller hung up without leaving a message.

She dipped her brush into the paint. Her nails, her fingers, were coated in the stuff. More work for her manicurist who had taken to joking that she was going to finance a Christmas holiday in the Caribbean with all the extra money she was making.

The phone began to ring again. She dropped the brush, slid down the stepladder, grabbed the phone before the machine could pick up.

'Yes?' she gasped breathlessly. 'I'm here.' There was the briefest silence. Then once again the caller hung up.

Fingers shaking, she punched in 1471. Listened to the recording telling her that '...we do not have the caller's number...'

She rubbed briskly at her arms, stippled with gooseflesh. Of course she was cold. She'd opened the windows... What she needed was a warm drink, a hot mug to wrap her fingers around.

She'd just reached the kettle when the phone rang again. She grabbed the receiver fastened to the kitchen wall and said, 'Please don't hang up!'

'Belle?'

Ivo.

'Oh...'

'Not who you were expecting, evidently.'

'No… Yes…' She shook her head, which was pretty point-less since he couldn't see.

She should have guessed he'd ring.

He'd called at the flat earlier: she'd looked out of the window and seen his car—not the work day Rolls with Paul at the wheel, but the big BMW he drove himself—and had resolutely ignored the doorbell.

This was hard enough without these constant reminders of everything she was missing. Not just the scent of him that nothing seemed to eradicate, but the way he loosened his tie, undid the top button of his shirt, without even realising what he was doing. The way his hair slid across his forehead, evoking memories of it damp, tousled from the shower…

'Are you still there?'

'Yes. Sorry. I'm waiting for someone to ring,' she said helplessly.

'I got that bit.' He didn't wait for her to reply but said, 'You sound as if you've just run a marathon.'

'Nothing that easy,' she said. Then, a touch desperately, 'Can this wait?'

'It's okay, I won't stop you working. If you'll just buzz me up…'

Buzz him up? She looked at the phone, then put it back to her ear. 'Where exactly are you?'

'Right this minute? Standing on your doorstep.'

She crossed to the tall French windows, standing open to the small balcony to let out the smell of paint, and looked down. There was no BMW parked at the kerb behind her own smart little convertible. Only a van.

Clearly he'd guessed she was lying doggo earlier so this time he'd stopped further down the street and used his cellphone to establish that they both knew she was in before he revealed his presence. Smart.

'I'm really busy,' she said. 'Can't you just push the post through the letterbox?'

'The stuff I've got here won't go through the slot.'

Which was why he'd had to come back. Now she just felt bad and, out of excuses, she buzzed him up, but, having left the flat door open, she abandoned all thoughts of making a hot drink and retired to the top of the stepladder, ensuring a safe distance between them. If he saw she was working, he'd get the message and wouldn't linger.

She heard him walking across the bare boards in the hall. 'Just dump it there,' she called, hoping he'd take the hint.

'One more load.'

What?

She frowned, turned, too late. She could hear him taking the stairs two at a time.

One more load of what?

Had he got tired of waiting for her to pick up her belongings and decided to bring them over?

She swallowed down the painful lump in her throat. This was her decision. She should be grateful, she thought, jabbing at the cornice with her paintbrush. He was saving her a job.

She heard him put something down. 'That's it.'

'Could you leave it in the hall?' she said, aware that he was watching her but resolute in her determination not to get drawn into conversation. To even look at him.

'It won't be much use there.'

And he had her. Curiosity…

Ivo had a weekend wardrobe to go with his weekend car. Expensive casuals, cashmere sweaters. He might carry on working at the weekend, but he didn't consider it necessary to wear a suit when he was at home. Mostly.

Today he was wearing stuff she'd never seen before.

Really old form-hugging jeans that clung to his thighs and sent a whisper of heat whiffling down her spine. And, under a rubbed to the nap leather bomber jacket, a T-shirt that had once been black but was now so faded that even the logo promoting some eighties' rock group was barely discernible.

She tore her gaze away from his body to look at the box he'd set on the floor. It contained not post, not clothes, but paintbrushes, brush cleaners, sandpaper —tools a decorator might use.

Startled, she said, 'What on earth do you think you're doing?'

'The ceiling will take half the time with two of us doing it. I've brought my own stepladder,' he added, before she could tell him that he wasn't sharing hers.

While she balanced, open-mouthed, inches from the ceiling, he fetched it from the hall and set it up in the far corner of the room. Then he took a paint kettle from the box, helped himself to paint from the tin she was using and, without waiting for her to thank him, or tell him to get lost, he set to work.

'No,' she said, when her mouth and brain finally reconnected. 'Stop.'

He paused. Glanced across at her.

This was too weird. Ivo didn't do this stuff. If something needed fixing, Miranda summoned someone from her list of 're- liable little men' to deal with it.

'Haven't you got more important things to organise? A take- over, a company launch or something,' she added a little des- perately.

He almost smiled. 'All of the above, but I can spare a couple of hours to give you a hand with this,' he said, then carried on with what he was doing.

No doubt. Leaving some CEO to sweat out his future while he calmly painted her ceiling as if he had nothing more on his mind than…painting her ceiling.

'No,' she repeated, putting down her paintbrush and climbing down the ladder. If he had time to spare he could go 'spare' it somewhere else.

She didn't want him turning up, taking over. This was like the thing with the car. Treating her as if she didn't know what she was doing. This was her life and she could handle it.

He took no notice, carrying on as if she hadn't spoken. For a moment she stood beneath him, watching as he stretched to stroke the brush across the ceiling, apparently hypnotised by the bunching and lengthening of the muscles in his arm. The low autumn sun slanting in through the window gilding the fine sprinkling of dark hairs on his forearm.

'If you've got an hour or two to spare,' she said, dragging herself back to reality, 'world peace could do with some attention.'

'I can do a lot more with ethical company practice than I could ever manage with political hot air.'

'Can you?' Then, because getting into a debate with him was not her intention, 'How did you know I'd be decorating?'

He stopped, looked down at her.

'I noticed the colour cards on Monday and when I came by earlier you'd taken down the curtains.' He dipped the brush into the paint. 'It seemed like a reasonable assumption.'

'I might have had decorators in.'

'You have,' he agreed. 'Grenville and Davenport. No job too small.'

How easy it would be to let that go. Just shut up and let him get on with it. Working towards each other. A team. This was, after all, what she had always wanted. The two of them getting close over the ordinary things that other people did.

People, courtesy of the gossip magazines, thought she had the perfect life with Ivo, but she would have willingly surrendered the luxury just to fall into bed with him at the end of a hard day, too tired to do anything but sleep.

'If you want to set up in the decorating business, Ivo, you're going to have to find another partner. And somewhere else to practise.'

Ivo, who had relied on speed and determination—skills that had served him well in the past—to override her initial objections, certain that in retrospect she'd be glad of his help, stopped what he was doing, finally listened to her.

'You really mean that, don't you?'

'I really mean it.'

'You don't want my help?'

'I don't want anyone's help. I want... I need to do this myself.'

He didn't just listen to her, but heard what she was saying. Understood that she wasn't rejecting him. She just wanted to do it herself. To prove something to both of them.

It was a light bulb moment.

'You'll be sorry,' he said. He was sorry too, but only for himself. There was something about Belle's new determination, new independence that made him intensely proud of her.

He climbed down the ladder, looked around. 'This is a lovely room. Good proportions.'

'It will be when I've finished. When the new carpet is down.'

He looked at the tacks and staples, the junk left behind by earlier floor coverings. 'These should come up.'

'It's on the list.'

'Do you want me to leave the tools?'

Belle, looking down, caught a glimmer of something in Ivo's grey eyes. Need? Could it really be need? It was so swift that she couldn't be sure, only that it made her regret her swift rejection. To be needed by him was all she had ever really wanted.

And she'd made her point, she rationalised.

That if he stayed it would be on her terms, not because she couldn't cope. Not even because he thought she couldn't cope. And, as he sorted out pliers, a small hammer, a screwdriver, she said, 'On the other hand, I suspect it's going to be a tedious and painful job. Nail hell.'

'Painting a ceiling isn't much fun,' he pointed out. But he left her to it while he began to tackle the floor.

The phone rang three more times while they were working.

The first time Ivo looked, but made no effort to get up. The caller hung up without leaving a message.

The second time it rang he said, 'Do you want me to get that?'

'No, thanks,' she said. It was another hang-up.

The third time they both studiously ignored it.

When she was done, she climbed down the ladder, her fingers so stiff she could barely move them. He didn't say a word, simply took her brush and the one he'd briefly used and washed them out under the tap. She didn't protest since the alternative was standing shoulder to shoulder with him at the sink. That was when the phone rang for the fourth time.

'Do you get a lot of hang-ups?' he asked, turning to her. 'This is an unlisted number?'

'It's nothing. One of those computer things,' she said. 'A silent call. I'll contact the phone people. You can register to put a stop to them.'

'Silent calls don't listen to the answering machine message,' he pointed out. 'They hang up as soon as the phone is answered.'

'Do they?'

'It sounds to me as if someone likes listening to your voice.'

'What?' Then, blushing, 'What are you suggesting?' she demanded.

'Nothing.' He squished more soap on to the bristles. 'Only that you might consider changing your number.'

'I can't...' she began. Too vehemently. 'I can't be bothered. It's too much trouble to let everyone know.'

'Well, so long as it stops at hang-ups. Nuisance calls can get nasty. Who knows you're living here on your own?'

She shrugged. 'Not many people. My agent. You.'

Daisy...

Could it be Daisy calling just to listen to her voice? Building up courage to get in touch...

'And someone else,' he suggested, working the soap into the bristles with his long fingers, although the brush looked pretty clean to her. 'I've been expecting to read all about this...' he made a gesture with his head that indicated the flat '...in the newspapers.'

'Have you? Yes, well, it's a smoke and mirrors thing. The new image has distracted them for the moment.'

That and the fact that the split had all been so unbelievably civilised. There had been no drama. No tears. No sordid triangle spilling out into the public arena. Nothing to draw attention to what had happened.

The flat below her was between tenants and her ground floor neighbours, if they had actually noticed her comings and goings, presumably thought she was just doing some work on her empty flat.

It was almost as if the idea of her leaving Ivo was so unbelievable that while the world, if it looked, must plainly see what had happened, it collectively refused to believe its own eyes.

'Better make the most of the breathing space,' she advised him. 'It'll happen soon enough.' Then, because he had to find out sooner or later, 'With luck my other news will save you from the worst of it.'

He stilled.

'Other news?'

'My departure from breakfast television.'

'What?'

'Welcome to the club.' He raised his eyebrows. 'The "What?" club,' she said, making little quote marks with her fingers, although he'd sounded surprised rather than shocked, which had been the standard response. As if he'd been anticipating something different, although if he really thought she was having an affair why would he be here today, helping her decorate? Presumably that would be the 'lover's' prerogative. 'So far the membership is pretty exclusive. The network executives. My agent. When the news breaks I imagine it'll be standing room only.'

'Undoubtedly. Breakfast will never be the same again. Have they got anyone else lined up?'

Was that it? Mild surprise and who's taking over from you?

'For the moment they're refusing to believe it,' she said. Rather like his response to the fact that she'd left him. 'They think I'm angling for more money.'

'And are they offering it?'

'I'm getting the impression that I can pretty much fill in the blank, which is ridiculous. No one is irreplaceable.'

'You think?' For a moment she thought he was going to say more, but he let it go. 'Do you have anything else lined up?'

'I'm taking a break. It's not for the want of offers,' she added. Pride talking. 'Including a six-figure advance for my biography.' It would be ghost-written, Jace Sutton, her agent, had assured her, assuming that her horrified response was due to the thought of having to put pen to paper herself.

'I'd save that one for the pension fund.'

'Don't panic; I have no intention of washing my dirty linen in public.'

'What dirty linen would that be?'

'Nothing,' she said quickly. 'It's just an expression. Neither do I see myself as the host of a daytime game show.'

'What about that project you're working on?'

'Project?'

'Something about adoption?' he prompted, regarding her with a look that left her floundering.

How did he know?

'You were researching the subject the other day.'

'Oh, right. Yes.' She cleared her throat. 'It's in the very early stages.'

Actually not such a bad idea, she thought, recalling some of the stories she'd read. The desperate searches. The joyful reunions. The heartbreak of a second rejection. Maybe she could put together something that would really help people like her, like Daisy.

Realising that Ivo was expecting more, she said, 'Perhaps I should make producing my own documentary a condition of staying on. That would really test the network's resolve.'

He frowned. 'You're joking, surely?'

'Well, yes, obviously…'

'Unless they're complete fools, they'd jump at it.'

He thought that? Really?

'But why bother?' he went on.

Obviously not.

'If it's something that you're passionate about, you should set up your own production company.'

She stared at him.

'My own company?'

'If you're moving on, it's the next logical step. You could do what you wanted without the bean counters pulling the strings. If you're interested I'm sure Jace would know who to approach for finance.'

'No.'

She wasn't one of those high-flying women with a first from Oxford.

'Making television programmes is expensive,' he said, mis-understanding her response.

'I know, but who on earth would risk money on me?'

'People trust you, Belle. The public love you. I...'

His voice faltered and in a second the atmosphere had slipped from a relaxed working relationship to something else as heat, like the opening of an oven door, flared between them.

'You?'

'I should be going.'

CHAPTER FIVE

HE'D nearly blown it. Ambushed by a four-letter word that he didn't know the meaning of.

After her initial rejection of his help, he'd been so careful to keep it casual. Didn't even know what was driving him to hang in there when he understood only too well why she'd left him. He had, after all, been waiting for the moment ever since he'd fled their honeymoon in an attempt to right the wrong he'd done her, intending to tell her the truth when he'd put it right. But there were some mistakes that were beyond repair.

Belle had been right to leave him.

It was just that he couldn't let her go. Winning her back was never going to be easy. He knew her; it would have taken far more than a fit of pique to screw her to the point that she could walk away from a marriage that, by her own admission, had given her everything she'd ever wanted. Bar one.

Marriage should have been the last thing on their minds. Somehow it had been the only thing on his and her terms had made it so easy for him.

'Marriage?' She'd laughed at the very idea. 'The only reaon I'd marry is for security. A man so rich that I'd never have to think about money for the rest of my life. Never have to worry about whether the network were going to renew my contract...'

And he'd said, 'So, what's your problem? Just say the word and I'll buy the network.'

'What about love? Don't you…?'

'We're adults, Belle. Love is for adolescents.'

'But why marriage?' she'd pushed.

'It keeps the taxman at bay.'

It had been that easy. Too easy…

He should have known that nothing good was ever won that lightly and now he was going to have to put in the hard work.

Easier said than done. He was so bad at the emotional stuff.

It was second nature to Belle. She could reach out, touch people. She'd done it to an entire country for heaven's sake; he'd turned to look at her out of curiosity, never suspecting the danger. Certain that he was immune.

Ivo had always prided himself on total honesty in business, but obsessed with her, with the need to own her, keep her for himself, he'd behaved like the worst kind of corporate raider, taking advantage of her vulnerability, her insecurity, instead of digging for its cause. Sweeping her away on the promise, the one thing that he could offer her, that, as his wife, she'd be safe from the vagaries of an uncertain business.

He'd just thanked his lucky stars that she hadn't asked for more and for a whole week had lived in the bliss of a happiness he'd thought beyond him. Bliss that had been shattered when, in the sleepy aftermath of intimacy, she'd babbled happily about a future that he'd never envisaged. A rose-coloured picture of family life that he knew did not exist.

He should have told her the truth then. Given her the choice of walking away. But he couldn't risk losing her. Any more than he could let her walk away now.

Useless at emotion, he'd utterly blown his first attempt to keep her from leaving him. Now he was using what he knew, the techniques he'd learned in the boardroom, in an attempt to save his marriage. It was, he'd rationalised, not that different from planning a takeover, albeit one that might turn hostile at any moment.

The first requirement was information. He needed to know what she was thinking. What was driving her.

Had she, out there in the Himalayas, pushing her body to the limit, reached deep and found a hitherto unsuspected inner strength? Was that why he'd felt so threatened by the trip? Why, from the first moment it had been mooted, he'd behaved like some Victorian husband demanding obedience from his wife.

Too late to see that he should have abandoned business and gone with her. Right now, all he could do was hang in there, show her that she needed him, whether she knew it or not.

Decorating, for instance. What on earth did she know about decorating? How hard it was?

He'd banked on the fact that she'd be grateful for the help and when he'd seen that she'd opted to the safer distance at the top of the ladder, knew that short of coming down and throwing him out this morning, she was stuck with him.

His first mistake.

But then, almost as if she'd taken pity on him, he'd got an unexpected reprieve and since then it had gone as well as he could have hoped. Better…

In fact it was just as well that his hands were still under cold running water. It would have been so easy to go with the moment, take it from there.

He had felt the reciprocal heat in that exchange, a charge that on any other occasion would have carried them to bed. This time, he knew, that wouldn't be enough.

A company, its directors, staff had to be courted, won over, to want what he was offering. He'd never courted Belle. What had happened between them had been instant, a conflagration.

Now, he sensed, he needed to go back to the beginning, do what he hadn't been able to do then. Keep his head. Be patient. Somehow make himself say a word that had been deleted from his dictionary. That he wasn't sure he understood. Except if the pain he was feeling, if the emptiness in his life had a word, then it could only be filled by Belle.

Easier said than done. It took a supreme effort of will to keep his hands from reaching out to her, keep them from cradling her face, from holding her as he slipped the buttons on her jeans.

Stopping her protests with his mouth as he dipped his fingers into her warmth, watching as her eyes darkened until the only thing on her mind was him, buried deep inside her.

Not this time.

Patience…

After what felt like a year but was probably no more than a couple of seconds, Belle looked away, took a step back and, before she could put into words what she was plainly thinking—that he should go—he said, 'I'll put together a package for you to think about.'

And, instead of suggesting he pick up some sandwiches and coffee from the café across the road, he stuck to the practicalities.

'Do you know how to prepare the woodwork?' he asked.

'Pre…prepare…' She took a breath and the fact that she was forced to swallow before she could speak gave him hope that she had felt the same urgency, the same need. 'Wash with soft soap, sandpaper, undercoat, gloss,' she said quickly.

'You always were hot on preparation.'

People thought that she winged it on her programme every morning, that the apparently off-the-cuff chatter came easily. He knew the hours she put in every day, studying the people she was going to interview, the subjects she was going to cover, so that it looked that way.

'The woman in the shop gave me a leaflet explaining it all.'

'Right. Well, I'd better be going.'

'Thank you for your time. My manicurist will be eternally grateful,' she said, easing her neck.

He clenched his fingers into his palms to stop himself reaching out to knead out the creases. Patience…

'If you need anything—'

'I can manage.'

'I can see that.' Then, 'You've got an awards dinner on Tuesday?'

'Yes.' She pulled a face. 'I didn't think you'd remember.'

'It's in my diary. I've told Manda you'll be picking up some of your stuff. Or is there going to be a new dress to go with your new look?'

'I've already invested in a very old one. I'll pick it up after work on Monday, if that's convenient?'

While he was at the office. 'Manda should be home. If not, you've got your key.' Then, fighting the urge to offer himself, 'You have an escort?'

'Jace offered…'

He nodded. Her agent's presence at her side at the biggest industry event of the year wouldn't raise any eyebrows. 'Paul is free for the evening so if you'd like him to drive you—'

'No,' she said quickly. 'Thank you. I've made my own arrangements.'

He dug in his pocket for his keys, just about managing to stop himself from saying any of the things that were fighting to trip from his tongue. Keep it to a casual, 'Fine. Well, good luck.'

'Thank you.'

So formal. So distant. And, before he knew it, he was standing beside the van he'd borrowed from the office janitor.

He glared at her convertible. It was a declaration of independence. Of separation. He wanted to have it towed away, put in a crusher, reduced to a cube of metal. But what good would that do? Belle had made it very clear that it was her business, not his and maybe he should be taking notice of that. Give her space to stretch her wings. Test herself. Doing what his sister had been so incapable of. It occurred to him that he should be helping her find her feet, not trying to knock her off them, keep her dependent upon him.

He had intended to turn up tomorrow, find something else to do. Maybe he needed to wait for her to ask for his help.

As he rounded the van to the driver's door, he realised he wasn't the only one looking at it as if it were a hate object. A girl, stick-thin, her fair hair streaked with green and wearing clothes a charity shop would shun, was glaring at it too. It undoubtedly represented everything she didn't have and he wondered if she was planning to break in or just take out her envy on the immaculate bodywork.

'What are you staring at?' she shouted when she saw him looking at her.

'My wife's car.'

Belatedly he realised how possessive that sounded. Belle did not belong to him. He did not own her.

He transferred his feelings of protection to her car.

'If you were thinking of breaking into it, I'd advise you to think again,' he said.

For a moment the girl defiantly stood her ground before, quite deliberately placing a hand on the door and setting off the alarm. Only then did she turn and flounce away.

Belle appeared at the window. She said something but, although her mouth was moving, the words were obliterated.

He mimed an instruction to toss down her keys so that he could kill the alarm and, by the time she'd joined him, it was all over.

'I hope that isn't going to happen every time someone gets within breathing distance,' she said.

'No. It was just some girl with green hair wanting to make an impression,' he said. He reset the alarm, locked up and handed back her keys.

'Take care, Belle,' he said, then, with the briefest touch to her arm, he climbed into the van. He drove around for a while, hoping to spot the girl. There had been something about that little scene that had seemed…staged. He didn't believe in it any more than he believed in Belle's documentary.

Her twitchiness when she'd thought he was looking at her laptop last week, the way she'd jumped when an email arrived, had suggested something else entirely.

Something that might explain everything. That could offer him a measure of hope.

She'd been looking at adoption sites and one answer had leapt into his mind and refused to go away. If Belle had been a teenage mother, had given her baby up for adoption, the child could well be coming up to an age where it was possible to search for, contact his or her birth mother.

Was that what this was all about? Was she waiting, hoping for a call from a child she'd surrendered to a couple who couldn't have one of their own? How ironic that would be.

And he wondered too about those silent calls.

Her stiff back as she'd determinedly ignored them, the way her brush had stopped working as her invitation to leave a message came to an end, the beep. The slump in her shoulders as there was yet another hang-up.

Had her family disowned her? Did people still do that? It would explain why she never talked about them.

It would explain so much more than that.

But why she'd married him was not the issue.

It was the fact that she'd assumed he would disown her too, once he knew the truth, that she didn't trust him enough to share her secret, her loss, that was painful beyond imagining.

Awards dinners were not a new experience for Belle. She'd even been nominated before, although admittedly not for the top honour. But arriving on her own, walking down the red carpet into a barrage of flashlights without Ivo at her side was a very new, very lonely experience. One that her agent's presence did nothing to assuage.

Thank goodness for the dress. Strapless cream silk, worn with a bronze lace evening coat that hung from her shoulders to spread in a demi-train, brought gasps from the crowds gathered on the pavement to see their favourites arrive.

And at her throat she wore the choker of large freshwater pearls, each nestling in its own crumpled gold and diamond cup, that Ivo had bought for her birthday the year before. It was stunningly modern and yet as ageless as the dress she was wearing. She'd forgotten about jewels, would have gone without rather than call Ivo, but he forgot nothing and had sent his chauffeur over on Monday night with the contents of the safe. He clearly expected her to keep them, but she'd picked out what she'd needed for the dinner and sent the rest back, citing security.

The dress, the jewels, were not enough.

In front of the cameras she was fine. It was easy to reduce her audience to one imaginary old lady, nodding off in an armchair. In public, faced with real people, she always expected someone to shout, 'Fake!' To expose her. Show her up for what she really was.

Without Ivo's steadying hand beneath her elbow, Belle had to fight down the urge to run, to escape all those eyes, all those cameras, reach deep for a smile as she forced herself to walk slowly along the carpet, stop to exchange a word with someone she recognised, respond to the calls of the photographers and wave in response to the calls of 'good luck'.

Call back, 'Thank you', when someone shouted, 'Great hair!'

She even managed to blow a kiss directly into the lens of her own network's news camera as it tracked her progress.

She told herself that Daisy might be watching.

Ivo, she knew, would not be. Beyond the financial and political news, he had no interest in television.

He had, however, sent her creamy hothouse freesias with a card inscribed simply with his name.

Just 'Ivo'. Not 'Love…', or 'Thinking of you…'. Not his style. He had, however, written it himself. Had spoken to the florist personally. His PA would have sent a basket of red roses. Miranda, more imaginative, would have scoured the hedgerows for deadly nightshade—but they would have been exquisitely arranged.

Ivo had sent her freesias the morning after their first night together, when they'd made love as if the world were about to end. An odd choice—they were the flowers a man might have sent to his bride—but exotic hothouse blooms would have been too obvious and he had never been that.

She slammed a door shut on that thought.

It wasn't a romantic gesture she told herself. It was the gesture of a man who, when he wanted something, was prepared to take infinite trouble to acquire it. Knew how to make surrender feel like triumph.

She thought he'd let her walk away, maybe even be glad that she'd taken the decision, but he was there every minute of the day, not just crowding her thoughts, but physically present. Checking that she was coping. Turning up to help her decorate, even. And that confused her too. It was as if he was saying, 'I'm fine with this…', 'I'm just helping you move on…'

It didn't feel like that, though.

Or maybe it was just that she didn't want it to be like that.

Bad enough that she'd rushed home on Monday. She might have fooled herself into believing that it was Daisy she was desperate to hear from, but the disappointment when Ivo had not dropped by with her post, when he'd sent Paul with her jewels instead of coming himself, had been just as keen as the lack of a response from her sister.

Ivo was watching the news, knowing that after the serious stuff they'd show the celebrities arriving earlier that evening for the awards dinner. As Belle took Jace Sutton's hand and stepped from the car, looked up, smiled into a barrage of flashlights, he could scarcely breathe.

Had he expected, hoped that she might look a little lost? As if she was missing him? On the contrary, she looked utterly self-possessed. Stunning. And, as she turned to the camera, blew a kiss, he was the one who was lost...

There was a tap at the library door and, as he flicked off the television, his housekeeper said, 'I'm sorry to disturb you, Mr Grenville, but there's a police officer looking for Mrs Grenville.'

The evening was interminable. Ivo's absence was not remarked upon; in the self-absorbed world of television, Jace Sutton, full of industry gossip, secrets, made a much more entertaining, and useful, contact.

Dinner, endless awards, gushing speeches, washed over her in a blur. When the man who'd given her that first chance—setting her on the path that ended here—at last read out the list of nominees for the final award of the evening—Television Personality of the Year—then opened the gold envelope and smiled as he read out the winner's name, it took a moment for her to realise that the name he'd read out was 'Belle Davenport'.

That it was her.

That she would have to walk up to the stage and somehow thank everyone who'd ever so much as made her a cup of tea for making her success possible.

Far too late to regret wanting to prove to herself that she could do this on her own and wish she'd pulled a sickie.

It took a while to make it to the stage. So many hands reached out to her that could not be ignored. Eventually she mounted the steps, took the trophy, turned to acknowledge her audience and the room stilled.

She looked down at the trophy in her hand and blinked back tears that she'd been fighting all evening. 'This trophy has my name on it, but it isn't really mine. It belongs to everyone who makes Breakfast With Belle the kind of programme people switch on every day. Susan, who meets me at four-thirty with a cup of Earl Grey and a smile. Elaine, who works magic with make-up. No, honestly, it's true. I do wear make-up...' There was laughter. 'It's unfair to pick out names, but look at the list tomorrow morning when the titles roll. Every one of them should have their name inscribed on this award, because it takes every one of those people, doing their job behind the scenes to make me look good. It belongs to the people they live with too, their partners who are disturbed at four o'clock every morning and who never get a decent night out because we have to be in bed by nine o'clock every evening.'

'Lucky Ivo Grenville,' someone shouted and everyone laughed, giving her a moment to recover.

Ivo, standing unnoticed in the doorway watching her, saw her smile, too.

'Lucky Belle Davenport,' she said with feeling when the laughter subsided.

For a moment he thought she'd seen him, but then he realised that she was seeing no one. That she wasn't speaking for effect, but from the heart.

'Oh, Belle. What have I done to you?' he murmured. A waitress was standing within touching distance, but she didn't hear; she was totally enraptured by the woman standing on the stage.

'Some of you already know that this next week will be my last "on the sofa".'

There was a rustle, whispers, a shocked 'No...'

'It's time to move on, but I want to thank all of you for watching, for supporting me over the years. Please be as kind to who-ever takes my place.'

Belle, unable to say another word, simply raised her trophy in acknowledgement of the applause. In front of her was a sea of faces but there was only one who would have made this moment memorable.

And as if the need, so powerful, called up the man, she saw Ivo standing by the door, looking at her. The only person in the room not smiling. Not applauding.

She walked down the steps and, ignoring the outstretched hands, she walked towards him until the applause died away to silence and she was close enough to touch him.

Not an illusion conjured up out of her need, but real, solid.

He wasn't in evening dress. Fine rain misted his hair, the shoulders of his long overcoat, and belatedly she realised that he hadn't turned up to witness her big moment. That he was here because there was something wrong.

'What is it?' she said. 'What's happened?'

'Not here.'

And her stomach lurched as, face set, he took her gently by the arm and led her out of the banqueting hall, down the stairs and into the lobby, past photographers caught with their lens caps on. The doorman was waiting by his car and she was in her seat before they recovered.

'What is it?' she demanded again as Ivo slid in beside her behind the wheel. 'What's wrong?'

'The police are looking for you. For Belinda Porter. They went to the flat and a neighbour explained who you are, that you were probably at home with me.'

'I'm sorry…'

'No. I'm sorry to have ruined your evening.'

He was looking at her as if he knew, she thought. Knew that all evening she'd been fighting the need to reach out, find his hand. Then she realised that it wasn't his absence he was apolo-gising for, but dragging her away from the celebrations for the award she was still clutching.

Breaking away from a look that seemed to sear her soul, she turned away, tossing the thing on to the back seat.

'Has there been a break-in?' she asked as he pulled away from the kerb, into the busy late-evening traffic.

'No. The flat is fine,' he said, concentrating on the road as he eased his way across the lanes.

Of course it was. If it had been something that simple he wouldn't have bothered her; he'd have dealt with it himself. Or had Miranda do it for him.

'I don't understand. Nobody knows I'm living there.'

Only Simone and Claire. Simone's lost diary flashed through her head but she dismissed it. The address of the flat couldn't possibly have been in her diary...

'Just you, my agent...'

Daisy.

She felt the blood drain from her face.

Daisy was in trouble. 'What is it? What's happened?'

'They wouldn't give me any details, Belle. Just that someone admitted to A&E earlier this evening was carrying a letter with your name, your address and they didn't know who else to contact.'

'Hospital? But...' She moved her lips, did everything right, but no sound emerged. 'She's unconscious?'

'Apparently she collapsed in the street. They wouldn't tell me any more.'

'No...' She cleared her throat, tried again. 'No.' Then, 'I'm sorry you were bothered. I didn't want you...'

'Bothered.' He finished the sentence when she faltered.

Belle heard the dead sound in his voice. Well, what had she expected? 'I'm sorry.'

'So am I, Belle. So am I.'

Ivo steered the big car across the city with only the intermittent slap of the wipers clearing the icy drizzle breaking the silence.

She.

He hadn't said whether the person was male or female, but Belle had known. So it was true. She had a daughter.

He waited, hoping that she would tell him, trust him. Then,

glancing at her as he pulled up in front of the hospital, he realised that she was beyond that. That she was taut with anxiety, with something else. Fear?

He reached across, briefly touched her hands, which were clenched together in her lap, and when she looked up he said, 'We'll take care of her, Belle.'

For a moment he saw something flicker in the depths of her eyes, something that gave him hope, then, quite deliberately, she shook her head, moved her hands.

'There is no we. Thank you for coming to fetch me, for the lift.' She opened the door before he could get out and do it for her. 'I can handle it from here.'

'You may not want to live with me, Belle, but I'm still your husband,' he said, doing his best to keep the desperation from his voice. To stop her from shutting him out. This was not like buying a car. Painting a ceiling. He'd spoken to the policeman. He knew how hard this was going to be. 'I am still your friend.'

She did not look at him as she said, 'We've never been friends, Ivo.'

And with that she swung her legs from the car and walked away from him, picking up her gown as she climbed the steps to the entrance.

For a moment he stayed where he was, pinned to his seat by her words. Knowing that he should go after her, that she would need him, no matter what she said.

We've never been friends…

Was that the truth?

He'd wanted her body. Had wanted the warmth she'd brought to his life.

What, apart from a sense of security that she no longer needed, had he ever given her in return?

Even now, when she'd left him, when she'd plainly said that there was nothing in their marriage, nothing in him, to hold her, he was plotting and planning as if she were some company, some *thing* he wanted to possess, control.

Not a woman who, with each passing day, he admired more,

understood more, missed more. Who he knew he would not want to live without.

We've never been friends...

Her words dripped into his mind like acid, peeling away the layers of scar tissue that had built up since his earliest years, protecting him from pain, letting in light so that he could see that he'd been asking the wrong question. It wasn't what, how much, he could give her to bring her back that he should be asking himself; he already knew that there weren't enough diamonds in the world, or flowers, no penthouse apartment built that would do it for him.

She didn't want, need, possessions; she had all she'd ever need without him. But security wasn't just a well-stocked portfolio. There was a deeper psychological dimension to it, a need that transcended physical comfort, one which no amount of money could provide; that was the security she'd sought from him and which he'd failed so miserably to give her. Because for all his wealth, he knew his own emotional piggy bank was empty.

How did you fill a dry well?

Where did you go for something you could not buy?

The dilemma of a thousand fairy tales. What did he have to barter that was worth the heart of Belle Davenport?

As if on cue the phone rang, offering, if not an answer, another chance.

Belle ignored the ripple of interest that her arrival in A&E provoked.

She made herself known at reception, was taken through to one of the treatment rooms where a scarecrow of a girl was lying on the examination table. Thin, pale, wearing nothing more than a T-shirt, a pair of black jeans. Belle tried not to react, betray her shock, horror, but forced herself to reach out.

'Daisy?' she said.

The girl did not respond to her touch, refused to meet her eyes. She was nineteen, nearly twenty, but she looked so young, so pathetic, so thin...

She'd had this picture in her head of Daisy as a grown-up version of the little girl she remembered. Blonde, pretty. Happy.

A young woman with a family. Someone she could love. Who would love her. Not this sorry creature.

'Is she hurt?' she asked, turning to the nurse.

'The doctor couldn't find anything. No bumps, no bruises, no sign of self-harm.'

Self-harm? She swallowed.

'Is she anorexic?' She could hardly bring herself to say the word, but she needed to know the worst.

'She's pregnant, Miss Davenport.'

'Pregnant!'

'She just passed out. It happens, although it would be less likely if she was eating regularly, had a little TLC.' Then, 'I thought you knew her?'

'Yes,' she said. 'I know her.'

At least she thought she did, but there was no connection, no instant bonding, none of the emotional attachment that she'd anticipated, hoped for. But then, why would Daisy have any reason to feel that way about her?

'It's been a very long time since I've seen her,' she added, when the nurse continued to look at her, clearly expecting a little more. 'Are you admitting her?'

'This is a hospital, not a B&B.'

B&B? Bed and breakfast… 'She can't wait until morning for something to eat!'

'We're not an all night café, either.'

'No.' Belle flushed with embarrassment. 'I'm sorry. I can see you're rushed off your feet. I'll go and organise some transport, get out of your way.' She glanced at Daisy, but there was no reaction, no pleasure, no rejection, just a blank stare. 'If that's all right?'

'If you want her, she's all yours.' She turned to the girl, who had not moved, and said, 'It seems as if it's your lucky day.'

That earned the nurse a glare. She was clearly immune because she just said, 'Take it or leave it, but I need this room for someone who's actually sick.'

Daisy sat up slowly, lowered feet encased in a pair of scarred and muddy black sports shoes, then slid to the floor, picked up her coat and headed for the door without a word.

The nurse raised a rather-you-than-me eyebrow in Belle's direction. Belle shrugged and then, realising that she was in danger of losing her sister all over again, hurried after her.

'Wait.' Then, when she kept going, head down as she strode towards the door, 'Daisy. Please…'

'I didn't ask them to call you,' she said, without stopping.

'I know.' Belle hurried alongside her, struggling to keep up in her high heels and long dress. 'But I'm here. Look, just wait while I call a cab.' Daisy finally stopped, but still did not look at her. 'Sit down. Or get a cup of something hot from the machine. Chocolate. That will warm you…'

'I haven't got any money.'

'Take this.'

Belle turned. Ivo was standing behind her, extending a handful of change in Daisy's direction, but he was looking at her. After what she'd said to him, she hadn't expected to see him ever again.

Maybe that had been her intention. To drive him away.

'You left your bag behind,' he said, before she could ask. 'Jace came after you, but we'd already gone so he dropped it off at the house. Manda phoned me. She knew you'd need your keys.'

'I…yes.'

Only then did he turn to Daisy. 'We've met before.'

She didn't reply, just stalked off towards the door.

'When?' Belle demanded. 'When have you seen her before?'

'She's the girl who set off your car alarm the other day.'

So close. She'd been so close… 'You said she had green hair.'

'That was four days ago. And actually I think I prefer the blue,' he said. 'It goes with her eyes.'

'What do you mean by that?'

'Nothing.' Then, 'Hadn't we better go after her?'

CHAPTER SIX

THERE is no we...

She'd said the words in an attempt to drive him away and she suspected that he was using 'we' now in an attempt to show her how wrong she was.

He needn't have bothered.

Whatever happened they would always, in her mind, her heart, be connected for eternity—in the memory of every touch, kiss, the sweet caresses that drove every other thought from her mind. In those moments when nothing else existed.

'Belle?'

'Yes,' she said, catching her breath. Then, as they emerged through the sliding doors, 'Where's she gone?'

'Not far,' Ivo said with certainty.

Belle ignored the cynical undertone—he didn't understand, how could he?—and said, 'We've got to find her. It's cold. She's hungry...' She couldn't quite bring herself to say what else she was.

'She's there, look. On the other side of the road.'

Wishing she was wearing something more sensible on her feet, something more sensible full stop, Belle ran down the steps. Ivo was there before her. 'Get in the car.'

She took no notice, side-stepping him, lifted her skirts as she began to run.

'Daisy, wait...Where are you going?' she demanded breathlessly, dodging cars to cross the road. Just wanting to hold her, keep her safe.

Then, as Daisy paused and turned, instead of reaching for her, she found herself held back by a force field of anger so powerful that she took a step back.

'Why did it have to be you? You abandoned me!' Then, pitiably, 'I wasn't looking for you. I was looking for my father.'

'Why?' The word was shocked out of her. 'Why would you want to find him? He didn't just abandon Mum and me, he abandoned you too. Everything that happened was his fault…'

'Liar!'

'It's true!' And then, seeing Daisy's face crumple, Belle would have done anything to call the bitter words back. She'd been a baby when it had happened. She didn't have a clue. How could she? All she knew was that her mother had died, her sister had abandoned her. Who else was there for her but some fantasy figure of a father? What other hope did she have?

The rain had stopped but a raw wind was whistling down the narrow street and, shivering, desperate to make it right, call the words back, Belle fought back all the bad memories. If that was what Daisy wanted, if that was what she needed, then she'd find her father for her.

'We'd have a better chance of finding him together, Daisy.'

'Oh, right. Like you want that.'

'It's what you want that matters to me.'

Ivo pulled up alongside them, got out of the car and took off his coat, wrapping it, warm from his body, around her shoulders, as if she were the one who needed looking after. As if he were the only person in the world capable of doing it.

Maybe he was.

And she heard Simone's voice saying, 'Ivo could help you…'

She had no doubt that finding Daisy's father would be a lot more difficult than finding Daisy. That if anyone could do it, he could.

She shook her head. She had to do this on her own. Stand on her own two feet and, shrugging off his coat, she draped it around her sister.

'I'll help you, Daisy,' she said. 'Whatever you want. There are agencies who can help, who specialize in searching for people. Family members.'

'Family? You're not my family!'

Ivo saw Belle flinch as if struck. Open her mouth as if to speak but unable to find words to express her feelings, and he felt her pain to the bone.

'Belle... Please,' Ivo said, impatiently. 'Both of you. Daisy? Why don't you get in the car?'

Daisy told him in words of one syllable, just what he could do with his car.

'There's no point in standing here getting soaked,' he said, letting it go. There was enough raw emotion flying about without him adding to the mix. Belle had made it more than clear that she wanted to deal with this herself, didn't want him involved. 'I'll leave you to talk.'

'Why would I want to talk to her? She abandoned me, left me, didn't want to know!'

'No!'

Belle's cry tore at him. He'd heard enough and cutting off the torrent of abuse that Daisy unleashed upon Belle, he said, 'That's it. Enough. I'll give you money for food, but I'm not going to allow Belle to stand here in the rain listening to your self-pitying rant—'

'Allow me?' Belle turned on him, blazing with fury. 'Allow me?'

'You won't be use or ornament with pneumonia,' he pointed out, doing his best to keep things on an even keel, but aware that sympathy would only fuel whatever was driving Daisy's misery.

'Don't you understand? I don't care about myself. I only care about her.'

'I know, Belle. Believe me, I know.'

'This isn't about you. About us,' she said, misunderstanding his meaning. Assuming he was referring to the fact that she'd left him for this. 'If I walk away, where will she go?'

'The same place she stayed last night, I imagine,' he said,

as gently as he could. 'And the night before that. Why don't you ask her?'

'No.' Belle felt the rain soaking through the lace and silk to her skin. Freezing rain. She'd been here before. Cold, wet, hungry. She knew all the dark places where frightened women hid from the night. 'No,' she said, talking to herself as much as Ivo, 'I can't take that risk.'

'What risk?' He turned his attention to Daisy. 'She's been hanging around your flat, ringing your number. Do you imagine it was a coincidence that she conveniently passed out in the street with your address in her pocket on the biggest night of your year? She's making you run, Belle, making you chase her. She's not going anywhere you won't find her.'

'What made you such a cynic, Ivo?' she demanded.

Ivo was desperate. The rain was coming down steadily now, soaking into the sweater he was wearing, soaking into the girl's miserable clothes, plastering Belle's beautiful dress to her skin and her hair to her cheeks, her neck. She said she didn't care about herself but *he* did and, despite everything, he cared more than he would ever have believed possible about her daughter too, simply because she was Belle's flesh and blood.

'I'm not a cynic, Belle,' he said, but he knew what he was dealing with here and if he had to be the bad guy to get them somewhere safe and warm, he was prepared to do that for them both. 'I'm a realist.' He opened the rear passenger door and said, 'What do you say, Daisy? A hot bath, a warm bed, good food. It's got to be better than this.'

'Stuff your hot bath. I don't need her and I certainly don't need you.'

'You don't get me,' he assured her, hoping that humour might work where an appeal to sense had not. She didn't move. 'Suppose I throw in a hundred pounds?' he offered. Money was the only inducement he had left. Money always talked.

'Ivo!'

'No? A thousand pounds?' he persisted, ignoring Belle's outrage.

'I hate you,' Daisy said, glaring at him. Then, sticking her chin out, 'Five thousand pounds.'

He saw Belle's face and something inside him broke. She didn't deserve this. She didn't deserve any of this…

'I hate both of you,' Daisy shouted, tossing off his coat, flinging it at Belle. It happened so quickly that while Belle was caught up in the coat and he was momentarily distracted, the girl disappeared. It was as if she'd melted away. Thin as she was, that clearly couldn't be the case; obviously she'd ducked down one of the barely lit alleyways between the buildings.

He swore, furious with her, furious with himself. It wasn't supposed to be like this. It wasn't how he'd imagined it. He'd been sure that when Belle had connected with her lost child, had that need fulfilled, he would be able to tell her the truth. From the time the policeman had arrived on his doorstep he'd known it wasn't going to be that easy but, with all his experience with Manda, he should have done better than this.

It was as if he'd turned into his father overnight.

'I'm so sorry, Belle.'

She shook her head. 'Help me, Ivo,' she begged. 'Help me to find her…'

Her words should have made him the happiest man alive, but life was never that simple. All he had to be grateful for was that he was there, that she was still speaking to him.

They searched the nearest alleyway, then the rest of the street, calling her name, Belle alternately pleading with her and yelling at her to come back.

It was only when her teeth were chattering so badly that she could scarcely form the words that she finally gave in, allowed him to take her back to the car. Even then she insisted on driving around very slowly so that she could peer into shop doorways, hoping for a glimpse of Daisy. She didn't bother to reproach him. She didn't need to say the words.

They both hated him.

Which made three of them.

He'd wanted to protect Belle, but all he'd done was hurt her.

It was the early hours before he insisted on calling a halt, not because he was ready to give up, but because she couldn't take any more.

'It's no good. I'm willing to search all night but if she doesn't want to be found we haven't got a chance.'

'You said that she wanted to be found.'

'She does, Belle. But maybe she doesn't know it yet.'

Belle's only answer was a long, painful shiver.

'I'll take you home,' he said, far more concerned about her than the girl who was causing her so much pain. 'I'll carry on looking. I promise I won't give up—'

'No, you're right. There's no point. She knows where I am.'

He didn't quite trust her quiescence but she waited patiently in the car while he fetched her bag from his house and, when they reached Camden, since she was shaking too much to connect key to lock, she surrendered it to him. He didn't wait for an invitation, but followed her upstairs, turned up the heating and put on the kettle while Belle got out of her finery, now damp and muddied around the hem, and into a warm dressing gown.

'Heat, a hot drink,' she said as she curled up on the sofa and he placed a warm mug of chocolate liberally laced with brandy into her hands. 'Daisy won't have that.'

'Her choice. She could have been here, Belle, but she wants to punish you. Wants to make you suffer,' he said, kneeling in front of her so that he could wrap his own hands around hers on the mug to stop them from shaking. Holding it while she sipped from it, not allowing her to push it away even when she pulled a face.

'She's not the only one. What did you put in this?'

'It'll warm you. Drink it.' Then, because he had to make her understand, 'She believes that hurting herself will cause you more pain than anything else.'

'How do you know that?'

'It's true, isn't it?' he said, avoiding a direct answer. She nodded. 'She'll come back when she thinks you've suffered enough. Tomorrow. The next day.'

'And if tomorrow is too late?'

She looked up, all colour had been leached from her face but she was still holding everything in. There were no tears, no outward display of anger. Coming from a family where emotion was repressed to the point of destruction, it had never occurred to him to wonder before at the way she held everything tight within herself—only to be grateful that she didn't indulge in tears and hysterics.

Now he understood where that restraint came from he would have welcomed a little hysteria, would have been glad to see the dam break, tears flow.

'She's so thin, Ivo…' He waited, hoping she'd let it all out. 'If I could just have given her something to eat. She needs care. Looking after. I don't have the first clue about where to find her.'

'What exactly do you know, Belle?' Then, because she was famous and wealthy and there were people out there who would use any vulnerability to take advantage of her, to cheat her, 'Are you even sure she's the girl you're looking for?'

'She had my letter. She'd registered with the adoption search agency and I wrote to her. How else would she know where to find me? My phone number…'

'You believed that was her calling, didn't you? The hang-ups?'

'I don't know. I suppose so. At least I hoped…'

'I'm sure you're right,' he said, rescuing the mug, placing it on a low table before moving to her side, encouraging her to lean into him, offering his own warmth as comfort. Doing his best not to think about the softness of her hair against his cheek, her scent seeping into his head, a yearning to draw her close and never let her out of his arms again. This was not about him.

This was about the woman he would do anything for. A woman who brightened every room with her presence. A woman he…loved. The word slipped into his mind, filling a vast empty space.

Belle, exhausted, let her head rest against Ivo's chest. Just for a minute. While she gathered herself.

He'd been so strange tonight. Loving, caring, awful. All mixed up. Like her. There had been that moment when she'd been so angry with Daisy for wanting her father. Proud of her when she'd challenged Ivo. Five thousand pounds? What was all that about?

'How many letters did you write?' he asked.

She caught a yawn. 'Letters? To Daisy? Just one.'

'I'm not talking about how many you sent. How many did you write?'

'Oh, I see. A few,' she admitted, remembering all the drafts.

'And what did you do with them? Have you got a shredder here? Or did you put them into the rubbish where anyone could find them?'

'No…' Then, 'No!'

Not 'no' to the questions, but 'no' to what the question implied. That this was a set-up, that someone had been through her trash, had found one of the drafts and was using it.

Ivo tightened his arm around Belle's shoulder as she pulled away, recognising in that cry of anguish a need that he couldn't fulfil.

All he could do was hold her, say, 'I know.' Be there for her. 'I know what you hoped for,' he said as her head fell back against his shoulder. 'It took me a while, but I knew there was something bothering you. Something that you didn't think you could share with me…My fault, not yours,' he said quickly. 'Then, when I remembered that you were searching for adoption websites, it all fell into place…'

'Ivo—'

'Tonight,' he said, before she could deny it, 'when I told you that someone had collapsed, you didn't ask who. You knew. You said "she". So…' Her eyes were wide, anxious. 'So I'm telling you that I know. You had a baby girl. Gave her up for adoption…'

'Daisy?' The colour had returned to her cheeks, she'd stopped shivering. 'You think that I…that she…'

She was finding it so difficult to speak that he said it for her. 'You've been looking for her. Tonight you believed you've found her.'

'Believed?' A sound, something between a shudder and a sigh, escaped her and she closed her eyes as if to blot out pictures in her head that were too painful to bear.

Dark smudges were imprinted beneath her eyes. How long had it been since she'd slept properly? he wondered. How long had she been searching? Longing? Why hadn't she come to him, asked him to help?

No, scrub that last question.

This was a marriage without emotional baggage.

They could have just stayed with the hot sex, two individuals who shared a bed, no strings attached. But Belle had wanted security and he'd just wanted her so they'd made a deal, formed a mutually beneficial partnership. Quite possibly the perfect match. They both had got what they'd wanted and, without any of those messy emotions, who was there to get hurt?

Too late to whine when he'd discovered he didn't like the answer.

'I know this is not what you want to hear now, but I have to ask if you're absolutely sure she's the girl you're looking for.'

He anticipated an angry reaction, expected her to shout at him, tell him that he didn't know what he was talking about, but, although her lips parted, the words didn't make it. She just pulled away from him as if touching him would contaminate her with the same vile suspicions.

It hadn't even occurred to her to doubt the girl, he realised. She wouldn't have checked or run any tests.

Maybe that made her a better person than him. It also made her vulnerable, at the mercy of the unscrupulous.

Right now it was more important that she trusted him and he gripped her shoulders, turned her to face him. 'Look at me, Belle.'

For a moment she resisted.

'Belle...'

Slowly, reluctantly, she raised her lashes. Her eyes were glistening liquid bronze, but still the tears did not fall.

'She didn't want me,' she said, as if that answered all his questions, all his doubts. 'It was her father she was looking for, hoping for...'

And that hurt more than he'd believed possible too. That out there somewhere was a man who'd given her what he was unable to—a child. A fool of a man who didn't know how lucky he was...

'We'll find her, Belle. I'll find her for you. I'll find him too, if that's what she wants. If she's really your daughter...' And suddenly he was the one having trouble getting the words out. 'If she's really your daughter, then that makes her mine too.'

'No!' Belle pulled away from him, wrenched herself from his arms. 'No, Ivo—'

No. Of course not. What kind of fool was he to imagine...? 'My responsibility, then,' he said, before she could tell him that it was nothing to do with him. None of his business. Said the words that excluded him for ever.

'No! Ivo, you've got this—'

'I've seen her, Belle. It's not going to be easy. You're going to need support. That's something I can do for you. I can help you both if—'

Her eyes widened a little at that, and this time all she could do was shake her head.

His fault. Exhausted though she was, she'd picked up on his hesitation. That word 'if'. *If* she's your daughter. If she wasn't some con artist homing in on a desperate woman. For her sake he wanted it to be so. For his own too...

But someone had to be responding with their head rather than their heart and it was so much easier for him. He'd never clogged his up with the silt of emotional cholesterol.

Hard though it was, as little as she'd thank him, as her husband, her friend, he was the one who had to lay it on the line for her. Even if she never forgave him. That was what you did for the woman you loved.

'She doesn't look much like you,' he said.

Belle blinked. 'Oh, I see. Yes, well, it's true that I haven't got blue hair.'

'Or blue eyes,' he persisted, knowing that she didn't want to hear this, that she wouldn't thank him for pressing this. Not now. Maybe later, when she'd had time to think, when her emotions weren't in a turmoil. 'It's not impossible, I know...'

'But you're suggesting that it's genetically unlikely?'

She was too calm.

'I'm sorry.'

'Why should you be sorry for pointing out the truth, Ivo? You're absolutely right.'

He frowned. The fact that she was agreeing with him did not fill him with optimism.

'But, then again, you're completely wrong.'

'Sweetheart…' The rare endearment slipped out. For a moment he thought she'd got it, understood the danger…

'Daisy is not my daughter, Ivo. She's waif-thin, looks like a kid, but she's only ten years younger than me. She's my sister. Half-sister, anyway. We had different fathers. Mine died, hers deserted. Same result.'

And for a moment he was the one momentarily bereft of words. Not?

Not her daughter?

He'd been so sure. And, without warning, there was a gap where some unrecognised emotion had briefly flared, lodged. An emptiness that had been briefly filled…

'She's your sister?'

'You sound almost more shocked,' she said.

'No…' He shook his head. It wasn't shock. It was far worse than that. 'No. I…' The words died.

'Don't feel bad, Ivo. You have every right to be shocked. She was all I had and I turned my back on her.'

He'd been so sure; now he was struggling to get to grips with this unexpected twist. 'But you were searching for her. I saw the adoption website.'

'She was adopted. I wasn't.'

'What? They separated you?'

'She was four. The perfect little girl. White-blonde curls, blue eyes. A smile that could light up a room. I was fourteen. An angry teenager who'd lived rough for the best part of three years, on the run from my mother's demons, from Social Services. Scavenging to live, seeing things that no child…' She shivered, did not resist when he pulled her back into his arms, rocking her as if she were the child. 'Daisy was whisked off to a foster family.

I was admitted to hospital with the same chest infection that killed my mother. A cough that a smoker would have been proud of. Hence the husky voice.'

He let slip a rare expletive as his imagination filled in the gaps. The reality of what she'd suffered.

'How did Daisy escape? The infection?'

'My mother gave what little food she had to us. I gave most of mine to Daisy. She was always warm. Always fed. Always came first.'

'And you did what you thought was best for her.' Not a question. More to himself than her. How could he doubt it? He'd seen the fervour with which she'd embraced her chance to do something for other children in that position. Understood now why the charity trip had been so important.

He'd always known that there was something in her past. It was too much of a blank; there were no links that went back beyond her time in television. No emotional ties. He'd thought that made them equal, but it didn't. She'd been loved once. Had been part of a family who took care of each other, made sacrifices to keep each other from harm.

He'd lived with her for three years and didn't know a thing about her, he realised, as the questions crowded into his head.

What had her mother been running from? Three years with two children, one little more than a baby. How on earth had they survived?

The only question he didn't have to ask himself was why she'd never told him.

But all that would wait. Some things wouldn't—not if he was going to find out if this girl was genuine. What had happened to her.

'The authorities separated you when your mother died?'

'Poor Mum. She was so afraid of Social Services. She knew that she'd lose us if they took us into care. Even when she was too sick to stand, she wouldn't let me get help. Then one morning I couldn't wake her. I knew she'd yell at me, tell me I was a fool, but I panicked, called an ambulance. I didn't want her to die.'

'You did the right thing.'

'No, Ivo. I should have done it a week before, when there might have been a chance. I wouldn't have cared how much she shouted at me. I would have run away from care to be with her.'

'You blame yourself?'

She roused herself, turned on him. 'Wouldn't you?' she demanded. Her lovely eyes, usually so full of warmth, life, were bleak with exhaustion. Something more.

He shook his head, unable to express what he was feeling, imagine what she'd been through. 'They shouldn't have sep-arated you.'

'Years ago they used to routinely split up entire families. Twins even. I've read some heart-rending stories, Ivo. Brothers, sisters reunited after half a century. It wouldn't happen now,' she said, reaching out as if to reassure him. As if he was the one who needed comfort. This was the warmth that her viewers responded to. She genuinely cared for people, even him, and he used that now, shamelessly, to draw her close, bring her back within the compass of his arms, as if he was the one in need of comfort. 'It probably wouldn't have happened then if there hadn't been such an age gap,' she said. 'Daisy was young enough to forget, have the chance of a decent life, Ivo. A real family. It was already too late for me.'

'It's never too late,' he said as another yawn caught her by surprise. She'd been on the go since before dawn and the warmth of the flat, the brandy-laced chocolate was seeping into her system, doing its job. She was both mentally and physically ex-hausted and soon she'd sleep, but she fought it, needing, he sus-pected, to get it all off her chest. 'I was so angry,' she said. Then shook her head, so that her short tawny hair, corkscrewed by the rain, brushed against his cheek. 'No. That's too clean a word. It wasn't anger; it was jealousy. I was jealous of a little girl who still knew how to smile. Knew how to make people love her. I couldn't forgive her for that so I walked away.' She sighed. 'Clever Ivo,' she said. 'You're always right.'

'No…'

'Oh, yes. You said she wanted to punish me and tonight she

did it in the only way she knew how, the way I taught her, by turning her back on me and walking away.'

'She'll come back.'

'Will she?' She looked up, seeking assurance. 'She said she was looking for her father.'

'You could help her. She knows that.' She shook her head just once. 'She had your address in her pocket, Belle. If she didn't want to know you, why did she keep it?'

Belle didn't answer, but closed her eyes as if to blot out a world of pain.

Ivo wanted to move mountains, change the world for her. Wanted to crush her to him, take that pain into himself, but he knew she would not, could not surrender it. That she was living in a world of guilt that only she could work through.

Power, wealth meant nothing here. For the moment all he could do was hold her, be there for her, no matter how many times she pushed him away.

Maybe, in the end, that was all anyone could do.

Maybe, for now, that was enough, he thought, as the tension finally melted from her limbs and, finally claimed by exhaustion, she softened into him, dropping away into sleep.

It had been weeks since she'd lain against him like this when, all passion spent, she'd fallen asleep in his arms. It was a moment he'd always treasured.

There was an almost unbearable sweetness in the way she surrendered consciousness to him and he felt a selfish joy in the moment—to be, if only for a moment, this close, this trusted.

'It will be okay, my love,' he said softly. Brushed his lips against her forehead. 'I'll make it okay.'

She didn't stir. His arm went to sleep. A muscle in his back began to niggle. He welcomed the pain.

CHAPTER SEVEN

SOMETHING hard and sharp was digging into Belle's cheek. She turned her head, reaching up to grab the pillow, turn it to the cool side.

Her hand encountered something—warm, firm. Not smooth cotton, but soft to the touch. Cashmere...

She'd fallen asleep on the sofa?

There was a blank moment as she groped for memory, then, as she shifted to a more comfortable position and a dozen niggles from back, arm, neck brought the hideous events of the night back to her in a rush, she opened her eyes, only to be distracted by the thought that the pashmina she'd draped over her sofa to disguise its age was not grey.

But then, as the fog of sleep cleared, it became obvious that she was not alone on the sofa.

She raised her head. Ivo, unusually rumpled, with a shadow several hours past five o'clock darkening his chin, was regarding her with sleepy eyes and she felt herself blush.

She'd slept all night on the sofa with Ivo, her head on his chest, her arm around his waist, their limbs tangled together and somehow the fact that they were both covered from neck to ankle in several layers didn't make it any less intimate.

Any less awkward.

She'd left him. She'd cut him out of this part of her life, had told him, more than once, that she didn't need him. But last night, despite the cruel way she'd rejected his offer of friendship, had walked away from him, he hadn't left her stranded without money or keys—which plainly she'd deserved—but had come to find her. Even when she'd turned on him, had blamed him when Daisy had run off, he'd spent hours patiently searching with her.

And when, finally, she'd told him the truth about her life, he'd stayed.

All night.

Of course the fact that she was lying on top of him, that he couldn't escape without waking her, might account for that. But he hadn't had to lie there and hold her as she'd finally succumbed to sleep. Hold her, whisper comfort in her ear. Call her 'my love'...

No. She'd imagined that. He didn't do those words. He was a minimalist husband. Beautiful to look at. Perfect in every detail. But cold...

'I'm sorry,' she said.

'What for?'

'Everything.'

For the fact that she didn't want to move, ever, but to stay pressed up against his warm body.

That she'd lied to him.

'For falling asleep on you,' she said, picking on the smallest reason. The one that wouldn't embarrass either of them.

'You'd have been more comfortable in bed, but I didn't want to disturb you,' he said, stroking a thumb beneath one of her eyes. Last night there had been dark smudges that it had taken some very expensive concealer to disguise. 'How long is it since you really slept?'

'I looked that bad?'

The phone rescued him—rescued both of them—jolting her out of a desperate longing to just stay where she was, in Ivo's arms, to forget everything else.

'What's the time?'

'Does it matter?'

'Yes.'

No…

She lifted Ivo's fingers from her face and for a moment just held them. How easy it would be to turn his hand, trail her lips along his fingers, enticing a response, a touch, a kiss, the slow peeling back of her robe, Ivo's mouth on her neck, his fingers trailing over her skin in a slow prelude to the closeness, the precious intimacy her body craved.

She'd missed him so much…

Realising that she was still holding his fingers, she twisted her head to look at his wristwatch. 'No,' she said. 'That can't be right. My alarm…'

'You might have forgotten to set it.'

'The studio! I should have been there hours ago. Why didn't someone call? Where's my BlackBerry?' she wailed, attempting to disentangle arms, legs.

'Still in your bag, switched off, I imagine.' She stared at him blankly. 'The award ceremony?' he prompted.

She groaned and, finally free, she jerked away from him, only to find herself hurtling back into Ivo's arms.

'Let me go!' she demanded.

He held up his hands. 'I didn't do a thing.'

'What?' She eased up, discovered it was her dressing gown trapped between Ivo and the sofa. 'Well, move!'

'My leg's gone to sleep.' He caught her arms, holding her. 'Calm down; whoever it is will leave a message.'

'No…' Didn't he see? Didn't he understand? 'It's Daisy! It's got to be Daisy—'

The machine picked up, her brief message played. The caller hung up.

'She was always going to hang up,' Ivo said as, not looking at him, she carefully extracted herself from the sofa.

She knew it, but it didn't help.

'It's a game, Belle.'

'No…'

A long, insistent peal on the front door-bell cut her off and, heedless of Ivo's warning, 'No!', she didn't stop to use the entry phone, but raced down the stairs in her bare feet, wrenching open the front door.

'Good grief, Belle, you look as if you've had a rough night,' Manda said, immaculate from the top of her sleek dark hair to the toes of the Manolos she was wearing on her narrow feet. 'It's just as well Ivo asked me to call the studio and warn them not to expect you this morning.'

He had?

'He did?'

When?

'Didn't he tell you?' Manda shrugged. 'He is here? I've brought him a change of clothes,' she said, lifting one hand, in which she was carrying a suit carrier and a document case. 'I'm sure your problems are much more pressing, but I've been apologising for cancelled engagements ever since you arrived home and since this one is with the PM—'

'I didn't ask him to stay,' Belle snapped, disappointment sharpening her tongue. Then, 'What are you talking about? What cancelled engagements?'

'Nothing important,' Ivo said, placing his hand on her shoulder, 'but you're right, Manda, I can't expect the PM to reschedule.' Then, regarding the paper carrier she was holding in the other hand, 'Please tell me that's coffee you've got in that bag.'

'Coffee and a muffin,' she said. 'Less messy than a croissant. You can eat while I'm briefing you on the way to Downing Street. I'll wait in the car.'

'There's no need,' he said, relieving her of the bag and the suit carrier. 'Save time and tell the PM yourself.'

'Ivo…' Miranda was, for once, the one left doing an impression of a goldfish.

'Do you have a problem with that?'

'You want me to go to Downing Street in your place?'

'He wants my help with some overseas aid project. If it goes ahead you'll be doing all the work. I'm just cutting out the middle man.'

'Yes, but…'

'I need you to do this for me, Manda.'

Belle sensed that this was important. That this kind of trust was something major. Something new.

'But...' Manda struggled for a moment with the idea, then said, 'Right...' She took a step back and Belle could almost see her giving herself a mental shake. 'I'd better, um, go, then.' Miranda glanced at her, then back at Ivo and said, 'I'll see you later?'

'Later,' he agreed.

She nodded once, turned, then, as she ducked into the back of the car Belle instinctively followed, stepping out on to the path to look up and down the street, hoping against hope to catch a glimpse of her sister loitering somewhere near.

'Don't,' Ivo said, taking her arm, drawing her back inside so that he could close the door. Then, presumably to distract her, he lifted the hand holding both his suit and the paper carrier and said, 'Coffee?'

'I don't think Miranda included me in the breakfast invitation,' she said, taking the carrier, looking inside. 'No, I thought not.'

'We can share.'

'The only thing we've ever shared is a shower and a bed.' And, last night, a sofa...

She turned away to run back up the stairs, into her flat, into the kitchen.

Damn, damn, damn!

Why hadn't he just gone with Miranda?

She'd left him. Didn't he understand? This wasn't his concern. And even when they'd lived together they didn't do this cosy breakfast stuff.

Then, as he followed, favouring his left leg, she forgot that and said, 'How is it? Can I do anything?'

For a moment their eyes locked and her mouth dried at the rush of memory. His thigh beneath her fingers. The warmth of his skin. The power-packed muscles beneath it.

'No,' he said abruptly. 'It's fine.'

'Right.' Then, as the silence stretched to snapping-point, 'I can't believe you just did that.'

'What?'

'Sent Miranda to see the PM in your place. You do realise that you've probably just thrown away a knighthood? Maybe even a seat in the Lords.'

'Do you think I give a damn?' he asked, taking the lid off the coffee, reaching for a couple of mugs, sharing the contents between them.

'To be honest, Ivo, beyond the bedroom I haven't a clue what you think.'

'About a knighthood?'

'About anything.'

'Then let me enlighten you about one thing. A couple of days ago I told Manda that she underestimated you.'

He did? No, no… 'I won't embarrass you by asking what she said in reply to that.'

'It wouldn't embarrass me, but I suspect Manda would never forgive me for telling you that you make her feel inadequate.'

Inadequate? 'I don't believe that.'

'As a woman.'

'They can do wonders with silicone these days.'

'It has nothing to do with the way you look. It's the way people respond to you. Your natural empathy,' he said. 'Which is why I did you the courtesy of assuming you wouldn't make the same mistake about her.'

It took a moment for Belle, momentarily floundering, to back-track. 'Oh, I don't underestimate her. I just think she'll scare the pants off the man.'

He looked up. Ivo was a man so contained that she sometimes thought she must have imagined the passionate midnight lover who came to her bed, who haunted her dreams. But here, in her tiny kitchen, unshaven, his hair, his collar, rumpled, the suspicion of a smile creasing the skin around his eyes, she caught a glimpse of the man who had laid siege to her, who had refused to take no for an answer and had flown her away to his paradise island for a sunset wedding for two at the edge of the sea.

'And your problem with that is?' he asked.

She shook her head and, ambushed by the need to respond with a smile of her own, ducked her head. 'No. You've got me.'

He took her chin in his hand, lifted her face and backed her up against the kitchen island, there was no escape. 'Have I?' he asked.

His fingers were cool against her skin. She shivered and somewhere deep in her throat a sound struggled to escape. She didn't know what it was. Yes or no, it would be wrong and she swallowed it down, shook her head, keeping her lashes lowered so that he should not see her eyes, read there what she could not disguise.

If he saw them, he'd know, as he'd known before when, across a room packed with people, he'd somehow forced her to turn and look at him.

Then his weapons had been flowers, tiny treasures, glimpses into his world.

But a man did not reach his heights without being intelligent, adaptable.

He'd seemed to accept her decision, but she should have known he would not, could not let her go that easily. This was now about much more than an unquenchable passion; his pride demanded that he win her back, restore his life to its ordered routine. Tempt her back in the gilded cage she'd stepped into so willingly. And he was prepared to go to any lengths to make that happen. Even using the infinitely more precious gift of his time, if that was what it took.

Even as she held her breath, there was a touch to her mouth so light that she thought she might have imagined it, that her lips, of their own volition, sought to confirm.

They met nothing but air and her eyes flew open but Ivo had already turned away to retrieve the muffin from the bag. He broke it in two, offered her half. Eve's apple, she thought. Persephone's pomegranate seeds. Like the touch of his lips, irresistibly sweet temptation...

'No...' Then, 'Thank you. I need to get dressed. I have to call the studio, make my apologies. Call my PR people.' She pulled a face. 'Heaven alone knows what the redtops will make of my rather sudden exit...'

'I'm sure Jace fed them some plausible story that will hold them off for the time being.'

'No doubt. It's what they'll do with it that bothers me.' Then, 'You asked Miranda to call the studio last night? What did she tell them?'

'That you had a family crisis. Jace and I both thought it would be better coming from her.'

'Of course. Who would dare question Miranda?' Before he could answer, she said, 'My life is about to get very messy, Ivo. You should step back.'

'On the contrary. You should come home so that you'll get some peace.' Then, with a frown, 'Is that what this is all about?' He made a circular gesture with half a muffin, taking in the apartment. 'Protecting me from tabloid splatter?'

'No.'

'You said that too quickly.'

'It wasn't something I had to think about.' If they'd had a real marriage there would have been no secrets and they could have taken 'messy' in their stride. 'You signed up for "perfect", Ivo.' For as long as perfect lasted. 'This was never going to be for ever.'

'No?'

She managed to pick up her coffee—it was a good thing that it was only half a mug or she'd have been in trouble—and tried to think of something to say. Nothing came and she had a momentary flash of sympathy with Ivo when, faced with her bald announcement that she was leaving him, he'd been monosyllabic.

Like him, she discovered, she didn't have the vocabulary to cover this situation, so she said, 'Help yourself to the shower in the guest room,' before retreating to the bathroom.

Ivo, left alone in the tiny kitchen, looked at the muffin he'd torn in half. It was in much the same state as his marriage. He fitted the two pieces back together, but there were bits missing and the join wasn't perfect; it jarred the eye.

But perfection was an illusion. Life had to be lived as it came with all its flaws and risks. Without the grit, there could be no pearl.

Belle was right. This marriage—this perfect marriage—was over. It was time to stop trying to fix it back together. What he had to do was work on rebuilding it from the foundations up.

Belle briefly recoiled from her puffy-eyed, bird's-nest-hair reflection, but had no time to worry about it. She certainly didn't waste time blow-drying her hair into her new style, just fingered it into place and left it to look after itself.

Her evening bag was on her bed where she'd thrown it last night when she'd stripped off her dress. She dug out her BlackBerry and switched it on, scrolling swiftly through a load of texts, all of them congratulations on her award. There were voice mails too. And a couple of emails.

Nothing from Daisy.

Well, what had she expected?

She opened the next best thing, an email from Claire. They'd had a lively exchange of text messages at the weekend; Claire had been putting off the moment when she faced her own demons and Belle had applied the cyber equivalent of a boot to her backside. She was hoping this would be good news.

It wasn't.

It was an email to Simone, copied to her:

I can't say I'm happy that my dirty laundry will soon be hanging out to dry in public…

What?

She flipped to Simone's email and she let slip a word she hadn't used in years. The lost diary had been picked up by a Sydney-based journalist who'd had no trouble in identifying all of them and had called Simone, inviting her to meet him. No chance that he hadn't read it, then. Every word.

She sat down, quickly thumbed in:

Simone, I've just picked up your email and can scarcely comprehend how difficult this must be for you. I'm with

Claire—you can tell Mr Tanner from me that Belle
Davenport thinks he's lower than a worm's belly—as if
he'd care! As for me, Ivo knows pretty much everything so,
as far as I'm concerned, you can tell him to publish and
be damned. Not so easy for you…

She thought about mentioning Daisy. Decided against it.

Then she returned the call from her agent. She owed him for
taking the trouble to leave the celebrations to deliver her bag to
Belgravia.

'Babe!' He was mellow. 'Anything for my favourite client. I
had a couple of calls from the diarists, but they bought the family
crisis. One of the benefits of being a good-living girl. If anyone
else had pulled a stunt like that, the press would be staking out
The Priory even as we speak. You might want to think up something credible for public consumption, though. The press being
what they are.'

'I've got credible. Whether you'll like it is something else.'

'Well, that depends. If it's something really shocking, I could
squeeze the publishers for another one hundred advance on your
biography,' he offered hopefully, 'and the papers would be
fighting for serial rights.'

'My financial adviser said I should keep that as the pension
plan,' she said.

'What about *my* pension? Thirty years from now I'll probably
be pushing up daisies. And celebrity biographies might not be
big business then. In fact, thirty years from now, if you don't
make a decision on some of these offers I've got lined up—or,
better still, sign that lovely new contract for your breakfast
show—no one will remember your name.'

'That's a risk I'm prepared to take. Look, I've got to go. I'll
call you later to fix up a meeting—'

'Come over now and we'll have lunch at The Ivy. Celebrate
the award. Better still, bring your financial adviser. He can pay.'

She laughed. 'I'll call you later, Jace.'

She was still smiling when she walked into the living room.

Ivo, hair damp, was standing back from the window, looking down into the street.

'You're still here? Haven't you got a corporation to run?'

'The shower was on a go slow.'

'Sorry. It's on my list of improvements.'

'It doesn't matter. I don't suppose it will collapse if I miss a morning.' Then, 'You might want to get your car keys.'

'What?'

He indicated the street below and she crossed to the window, standing beside him. Below her, on the pavement, standing next to her convertible, stood Daisy.

'Purple hair today. Oh, right, here we go,' he said as she looked up, and realising that she was being watched, took hold of the door handle and gave it a shake.

Belle was already running for the door when the klaxon sound of the car alarm rent the air. Was at the bottom of the stairs when Ivo caught up with her.

'Don't!' she warned, arm extended, palm face up as she held him off. 'Stay away. I want to do this.'

'You forgot the car keys,' he said, taking her hand, turning it over and placing them in her palm, wrapping her shaking fingers around them so that she wouldn't drop them.

'Oh…'

'She came back, Belle. She wants to see you. Needs to talk to you.'

'I…Yes…'

'Do you need me to stay?'

'I…' Despite her warning for him to stay away, she was suddenly scared.

He laid his hand briefly on her arm, then leaned forward, touched his lips to hers. Barely a kiss and yet it fizzed through her like electricity—pure energy—and for a moment all she wanted to do was reach out and grab him by the lapels of his jacket, pull him close, bury herself in his warmth until the world outside went away. 'You'll be fine.'

'Yes. Of course I will.'

'Call me if you need anything. You'll need someone to talk to. Someone you can trust.'

'Ivo, about last night…' As he opened the door, her words were drowned out by the car alarm and he turned to look at her. 'Thank you,' she said. He nodded once, stepped out on to the footpath, left her.

Goodbye…she thought.

Then, drawing in a deep, shuddering breath, she followed him out into the street where Daisy was leaning on the car, all aggressive angles as she watched Ivo remove a parking ticket from his windscreen—he'd overstayed the night-time parking limit—climb into his car and drive away.

The noise from the car alarm was deafening and Belle didn't attempt to speak above it, but unlocked the car, turned off the alarm, then relocked it.

'Neat car,' Daisy said. 'Can I drive it?'

'Have you got a licence?'

'Oh, forget it,' she said, stuffing her hands deep into her pockets and turning to walk away.

Belle, instinctively taking a step after her, was brought up short by Ivo's voice in her head.

It's a game. She wants you to chase her…

'I'm going to make breakfast,' she said and, hard as it was, she turned around and walked back inside, holding the door open. Then, 'A bacon sandwich.'

Bacon sandwiches had been dream food. Thick white bread, layers of bacon, ketchup… She'd been drawn by the scent to a small café that made sandwiches for office workers. Her mother wouldn't beg, but Daisy had been hungry and she'd picked a place, just out of sight of the café staff where she could lie in wait for customers, carriers stuffed with expensive calorie-laden sandwiches, coffee or hot chocolate in cartons with lids, huge muffins. Had learned to hit them for change while they still had it in their hands.

Guilt had done the rest.

It had been a great pitch, but it hadn't lasted long.

Someone had called Social Services. Or complained to the

café staff. Only her street-sharpened survival instincts had stopped them from being picked up but, even now, when she caught the scent of bacon cooking she felt something very close to pain in the pit of her stomach.

After a pause that felt like a lifetime, Daisy turned around and walked right by her and up the stairs without a word and was already standing in the centre of the living room looking around by the time her own shaky legs had carried her up.

'This is a mess,' Daisy said, looking around.

'I'm decorating.' The ceiling, one wall and the French windows so far—she'd needed to get the curtains back up—but all her own work. 'It'll look better when the new curtains and carpet arrive.'

'Are they beige and white too?'

'Please! The walls, when they're finished, will be Velvet Latte, the paintwork Silk Frost,' Belle said, hoping to raise a smile. Light, uncluttered after three years living in the Grenville family museum. 'It's minimalist.'

Like her marriage. Maybe it hadn't been such a good choice of look.

'It's boring. And no one has carpets now. It's all hardwood floors.'

'Not exactly neighbour friendly when you're in the top floor apartment.'

'I suppose.' Then, 'Your furniture is junk.'

'I'm going shopping for a new sofa this afternoon.' She'd picked out something ultra-modern in brown suede but she'd suddenly gone right off it. 'Do you want to come with me? Clearly I could do with some help.'

Daisy shrugged her skinny shoulders without taking her hands out of her pockets. 'Like I care what sofa you buy. You said you'd help me look for my dad.'

'We can do both. If that's really what you want.'

'You knew your father,' Daisy said, picking up the negativity of the question in her voice, turning on her. 'I never…' She broke off. Then, 'I never had anyone.'

'Mum loved you, Daisy.'

'She died.'

Belle swallowed down the words that leapt to her lips. Blaming Daisy's father for what had happened to them wouldn't help. They'd all abandoned her, one way or another.

'What about the people who adopted you? Didn't they love you?'

'They lied to me! I waited and waited and they said you'd come but you didn't. I wanted you, Bella, and you weren't there!'

Bella.

Daisy, only Daisy, unable to manage 'Belinda' had ever called her that.

'Where did you go?' she demanded and Belle, jolted out of memory, shook her head. 'Nowhere. A care home. Nowhere...' She shook her head. There was nothing to be gained from telling Daisy that her new family had only wanted her. That everyone had said it would be easier for her to settle down without disturbing memories of her previous life. She had known they were wrong, but no one would listen to her. And she'd been hurt and angry and grieving too.

She knew what Daisy was feeling now because she'd lived it.

'What happened to you, Daisy? Why are you living like this?'

'Like what?' Then, abruptly, 'I thought you were going to make breakfast.'

'I am. Do you want to come through to the kitchen while I cook?'

If she'd ever imagined this was going to be a joyful reunion, then last night had crushed that hope beyond recovery, but this was more difficult than anything she could have imagined.

Simone, Claire, she thought, I really hope, wherever you are, it's going better for you.

She took a pack of bacon from the fridge, turned just as Daisy swept something into her pocket. What? There was nothing on the counter top but a couple of mugs, the empty carton of coffee.

The muffin...

She bit down hard to keep the pain in, began to lay strips of bacon on the grill. 'Do you want to take off your coat?'

Daisy's only response was to wrap it around her more tightly and Belle didn't press it, but it took her a moment to compose herself. 'I'll find your father, Daisy.'

She just hoped the reality wouldn't hurt her sister too badly.

'Whatever. Can I use your bathroom?'

'Of course. Use the *en suite* in my bedroom.' The one in the spare bedroom was a bit bleak. Definitely on her list of improvements. 'First door on the left.'

CHAPTER EIGHT

IVO, uneasy, drove round the block, parked out of sight of Belle's apartment, bought a paper and walked into the small café on the far side of the street, ordered coffee and settled down to wait.

Belle had taken the unilateral decision that her past and their future were incompatible. That finding Daisy meant she had to lose him. That once the truth about her past became common knowledge—and the press, once they got a sniff of a story, would be digging around for every grubby detail—he wouldn't want to know.

That she felt that way shamed him.

Maybe she had wanted the security he could offer, but she'd wanted more than that. A real marriage. A family.

She wasn't the one lacking the courage to confront what that meant. He was the one who'd been incapable of embracing life with all its messiness.

He didn't blame her for leaving him—there wasn't a day in his life when he hadn't wished he could leave himself. On the contrary, he was grateful to her. He felt like a man who'd had his head yanked out of the sand. And Belle, still touchingly vulnerable, unsure, beneath the surface skim of professional polish, had broken out of her own shell. She was still vulnerable, still believed that her success was a fluke, the result of good PR, but she was making an effort to stand on her own feet, to do things for herself. Had been prepared to tell him that she no longer needed him as a prop.

In doing that, she'd kicked the legs out from under him. As they untangled themselves he had to make sure their feet were pointing in the same direction and somehow, he knew, Daisy was the key.

Daisy was gone for so long that Belle was afraid that she'd slipped out, disappeared again. Had to force herself to stay in the kitchen, watching the grill, sensing it was a trust thing. That she was being tested.

Her reward came when Daisy finally sauntered back in to the kitchen, smelling sweetly of vanilla-scented shower gel, her damp hair minus the purple streaks.

'Does he live here?' she asked, sliding back onto the stool, her look daring her to say one word about using the shower.

'Ivo?'

'*Ivo*! What kind of name is that?'

'It's a diminutive of Ivan. He was named for his Russian great-grandfather.'

'Lucky him. We don't even have a father between us.' Then, 'He said he was your husband, but there's no men's stuff in the bathroom.'

'He did? When?'

He'd said he'd seen Daisy outside the flat, but he hadn't said he'd spoken to her.

'He got all protective when I got too close to your car.'

'Oh.' She found herself smiling. Then, catching Daisy's 'yuck' look, said, 'He is. But we're separated.'

'Not that separated. He was here at the weekend helping you decorate. And he hadn't shaved this morning so I'm guessing he stayed all night.'

'Yes…' She could still feel the warmth of his kiss. Hear his soft, 'Call me…' 'Your fault. It was the early hours before we got back here last night,' she said, 'so he slept on the sofa.'

He'd got it so wrong! Thinking that Daisy was her daughter. But he hadn't been judgemental. Far from it. He'd said a child of hers would be his responsibility too. He'd hung in there, been there for her, even when she had been horrible to him. Would have gone out to continue looking if she hadn't stopped him. Then, when she'd fallen asleep on him, he'd stayed with her, holding her. All night. It must have been the first time they'd just slept together. Without getting naked.

Just like a real husband and wife.

She poured mugs of coffee, leaving the sugar and milk for Daisy to help herself.

'What about you?' she asked, pushing away the desire to do it again. Very soon. 'Are you living with your baby's father?'

'No.'

'Do you love him?'

'Oh, please!'

'You had unprotected sex.'

'There's no other way to get a baby.'

'You wanted…' She swallowed. Of course she did. Someone who would love her without reservation.

'She shouldn't have told you I was pregnant. That nurse. That kind of stuff is confidential.'

'She wanted me to understand why you'd passed out.' Wanted to be sure that someone responsible knew. Someone who would take care of her. 'Are you booked into an antenatal clinic? Getting vitamins? Have you been tested?'

'What is this? The Inquisition?'

'Your baby needs you to protect her. Keep her safe.'

'Like you would know all about that.' Then, 'I'll sort it, all right? I'm still getting my head around the idea.'

'How pregnant are you?'

'Totally. It's the only way.'

Her sister had a sense of humour. Things were looking up. 'I'll rephrase the question. When can I plan on being an aunt?'

'I didn't know I was pregnant until last night. I'm about six weeks gone, so somewhere between seven and eight months, I suppose.' Then, 'I didn't pass out on purpose, despite what Ivan the Terrible thinks.'

Belle struggled to hold back a smile. 'He's not so terrible. In fact he offered you five thousand pounds. Why didn't you take it?'

'He just wanted to get rid of me.'

'No…' The word had been an automatic response, but having thought about it, she said it again. 'No. He was just testing you.'

Protecting her. Treating her like some idiot who didn't know what she was doing.

'Then I guess I passed,' Daisy said.

'You don't have to prove anything to me,' Belle snapped. Then, 'Sorry. Late night.' And, changing the subject, she said, 'Okay. We can fix you up with a clinic. Go to classes together, if you like.'

'I don't need you.'

'Everyone needs someone,' she said. Someone to reach out a hand, to say '…Call me…'. Someone who you know will be there. Who cares how you're feeling.

How *was* Ivo feeling?

How had he felt when she'd told him she was leaving? Really?

She buttered bread, keeping her hands busy, but her mind needed total distraction. 'What about a job?' she asked. 'Or are you at college?'

'No.'

This was not going well.

She was paid ridiculous amounts of money to chat to total strangers every morning. She put them at their ease, made them laugh, drew them out with open-ended questions. The difference being that she'd done her homework on the people she interviewed. Knew the answers before she asked the questions, mostly. The trick was to avoid the obvious, get them to open up, forget the answers they'd prepared ahead of time and relax.

There was only one rule. Never ask a question that could be answered with a simple yes or no.

It hadn't occurred to her that it was a rule she would need when she finally came face to face with her sister. That a shortage of words would be a problem. On the contrary, she'd imagined that all the feelings would just come tumbling out. The anger, yes, she'd expected that, but had believed that the early years when they had been everything to each other, when she'd taken care of Daisy, looked out for her, would mean enough to override the years they'd spent apart.

It wasn't going to be that way. The wound had gone too deep and despite the fact that it would probably choke her, she bit into her own sandwich simply to stop herself from blurting out needy questions about her sister's life, the people who'd adopted her, knowing that she was just longing for answers that would absolve her of guilt, somehow justify what she'd done.

'Thanks for the sandwich.'

While she was still chewing through her first mouthful, Daisy had finished and she slid off the stool.

'You're leaving?'

Let her go. She'll come back.

That would be Ivo's advice, she knew. But then, detached, emotionally disengaged, that was easy for him to say. Much harder for her.

'Don't you want to stay and help me search for your dad on the Internet?'

'You think I haven't done that?' Daisy said, heading for the door. 'I'm not dumb.'

'I was going to contact an agency who specialise in finding people.'

For a moment she hesitated. Tempted. Then she said, 'What's the point? If he wanted to know, he'd be looking for me.' And she kept walking.

'Maybe he's scared, Daisy. Maybe he thinks you wouldn't want to know. Have you any idea of the courage it takes to seek out someone you've hurt? Let down?'

Her sister paused, glanced back from the doorway, her thin face wreathed in sudden doubt. But she rallied, said, 'Maybe he just doesn't care. Maybe he's just a...' She stopped, apparently unable, despite her defiance, to say the word.

'Say it, Daisy. It won't be anything I haven't heard before.'

'Babies can hear, can't they?'

Belle tried not to smile at this unexpected evidence of maternal care. 'So I understand.'

'You don't have any kids?'

She shook her head just once.

'Men are a waste of space.'

'Not all of them,' Belle said. Then, trying to keep the need from her voice, 'You can stay here, Daisy. There's a spare room. All the hot water you can use.'

'I've got a place.'

'Somewhere suitable for a baby?'

'I lived in worse when I was a kid,' she said.

'Then you know enough not to inflict it on your own child.'

'I was happy…' She snapped her lips shut, her lips a thin tight line.

Happy *then*? Was that what she'd been about to say? If that was her yardstick for happiness, what horror had she lived through since?

Belle shivered, but managed to hold in her concern. 'The offer's open. Any time.' Then, 'Do you need anything?'

'From my glamorous, famous big sister who couldn't be bothered with me all these years?' Belle caught the telltale sparkle of tears before Daisy blinked them away. Not so tough, then… 'I worshipped you.' Then, 'Not *you*. Belle Davenport. She was everything a big sister should be. Fun, warm, smart, caring and just so lovely. I used to watch her every morning and think if my sister had been anything like her I'd have been the luckiest girl in the entire world. Big mistake, huh?'

'It wasn't… That wasn't me.'

'Absolutely right. You're both fakes.'

'Daisy, please—'

'Please what? Fifteen years and all I get is a three-line letter and a photograph; what was I supposed to do, Bella…sorry, *Belle*? Fall at your feet in gratitude because you'd finally found time out of your busy life to remember that you had a little sister?'

'I never forgot you.' Belle stopped. What was the point? How could she expect Daisy to understand when she didn't understand herself. 'It wasn't your mistake, Daisy. It was mine.' Then, 'I'll

see what I can find out about your dad, so next time you ring…
don't hang up, hmm?'

'Who says I'll ring again?' she demanded, then flung open the
door and ran down the stairs.

Belle fought the impulse to go after her, to go to the window
to see which way she went. She didn't have any right to know
where Daisy went, who she was with. What her life was like.

She'd forfeited that when she'd walked away and now she was
going to have to earn Daisy's trust by being there for her. By
never, ever, no matter what, letting her down again.

Then, seized by a flash of inspiration, she ran to the window,
flung it open. 'Daisy! We can get a licence and I'll teach you
to drive.'

Her sister didn't stop or look up, just scrunched down deeper
into her thin coat.

Ivo, seeing Belle's front door open, folded up his newspaper,
stood up and made for the door. Daisy was always going to leave.
Assert her independence. Keep her sister guessing. Hurting.

He stepped back into the doorway when Belle flung open the
window, smiled to himself at her smart bid to grab the girl's attention. Not that Daisy responded. He'd have expected a self-
satisfied little grin, but instead she seemed to shrink.

He waited until Belle closed the window and then, keeping
to the far side of the road, set off after Daisy.

Belle, her own shoulders not exactly bouncing to her ears with
excitement, turned to her laptop and logged on to one of the
agencies that specialised in tracking down family members.
Somehow just filling in a form and pressing buttons seemed de-
pressingly impersonal; she needed to talk to someone…

Everyone needs someone.

'Call me…'

No. It was over. Not that he wouldn't help her on a practical
level. He was a man who could cut through red tape, make things
happen. But the cost was too high. Being with him was too

painful. She'd played the role assigned for three years, hiding her feelings, because the one thing Ivo Grenville had made clear from day one was that he never used four-letter words.

For a few brief days on that honeymoon idyll, she'd thought it didn't matter. That even if he never said the word, he lived it. Her mistake had been to let her guard down in the sweet, golden aftermath of love, when he'd been half asleep, when she'd been dreaming of a family of her own.

If his face hadn't been enough to bring her back to earth, the next day he'd left her to deal with some business problem that wouldn't keep—a sharp reminder of the status of honeymoons, of her, in his life.

She snatched her hand back from the phone.

She'd lived a half-marriage for three years and, while Ivo's passion hadn't dimmed, he had, if anything grown more distant, at least until these last few days. She loved him, had loved him since the day she'd turned to meet his gaze, fallen into those ocean-deep eyes. Would never love anyone else with the same wholehearted, body and soul commitment, but she'd take nothing rather than go back to the way things had been.

And she had Daisy to think of now.

She made a note of the agency's telephone number, then called, talked to an adviser who took all the details she had, somehow managing to tease stuff out of her memory that she didn't know she remembered. Or had, maybe, striven to forget. Promised to get back to her with something, even if it was to say that she'd found nothing, by the end of the next day.

That done, she poured out her heart to Simone and Claire in an email.

As she typed, she could hear their voices in her head asking all the right questions, posing ideas, offering suggestions. It was exactly what she needed to clear her head and she didn't bother to send the email.

There was nothing more they could do except offer sympathy—something she neither deserved nor needed. In fact, much as it pained her to admit it, what she could really do with just at that moment was a little of Ivo's detachment. His ability to distance himself from the emotional response.

Not that he was behaving in a wholly predictable way.

Turning up to decorate her flat had been completely out of character for a start. Calling in a professional—no, asking Miranda to call in a professional to do the job—that was more his style.

And cancelling business appointments? What was that all about?

Call me if you need anything...

She picked up her phone, flipped it open and called her insurance company and had Daisy's name added to her policy as a named driver.

Then she set about responding to all the messages.

Practical, unemotional. Ivo would be proud of her, she thought, except that his kiss had felt totally emotional.

Not in a big dramatic way. It wasn't a you're-hot-I'm-horny-come-to-bed kiss. It was an I'm-here-for-you kiss. A tender I-care-for-you kiss. She could almost have fooled herself that it was an I-love-you kiss.

If it had been anyone else.

She really should warn him about Simone's diary, she rationalised. There wasn't a thing they could do about it, but he'd at least be prepared for the fallout, the never-ending phone calls. Take action to avoid either him or Miranda being door-stepped by the press. Although, actually, she pitied any journalist who decided to take on Miranda.

She'd meant to tell him, but then Daisy had turned up and put it right out of her head.

It was time to bring Jace and her PR people into the loop too. Prepare a statement...

She flipped open the phone again and called up the address book. Then decided that Ivo had done enough chasing after her. It was time she went to the house, went through her things and sorted out what she was going to keep, what could go to a charity shop.

It was only when she stopped for petrol, to pick up a pair of L plates, that she discovered that her purse had been filleted like a kipper.

But for bones, read credit cards and cash.
Call me...
It seemed that she didn't have much choice.

'I'm sorry, Ivo. I'm so sorry.' Belle had said it a dozen times. 'I should have cut them up.'

She'd called him on his mobile and he'd come and bailed her out at the garage, then followed her back to the flat and was now sitting on the end of her bed, waiting for the call centre to answer while she checked to see what else was missing.

The only jewellery she'd had in the flat had been the choker and earrings she'd worn to the awards ceremony—precious only because Ivo had given them to her.

She'd abandoned them on the dressing table last night, not bothering to put them away.

Tempting glitter.

Her antique wedding ring was safe. Please let it be safe...

She opened the drawer in the base of her mirror, clutched at her stomach.

'Belle?'

She shook her head. It was too awful. She couldn't tell him...

'I meant to cut them up,' she repeated, just a little desperately. If she concentrated on the credit cards, she could blot out this, more painful, loss. 'Your cards.' She rarely used them. 'I should have left them at the house. If I'd been more organised—'

'I'm grateful that you weren't,' he said, hanging on, waiting in an apparently endless queue for his call to be answered so that he could cancel the cards.

'Grateful?'

'You wouldn't have called me if the only stuff she'd taken was yours.' She neither confirmed nor denied it. 'Would you?' he persisted.

'She's my sister.' Confronted with his impassive face, she said, 'Really.' It wasn't just that she'd called her Bella. 'There are things she said to me that no one else...' She raised her hand to her mouth, unable to say the words.

'Hush…' He reached out. Took it, kissed it, then held it, as he'd hold a child's hand, for comfort. 'It's okay. We'll get your stuff back, but I have to do this first. One call…'

'Get it back?' She tried to pull away but he closed his hand around hers, holding her a little more firmly, keeping her close. 'You aren't going to call the police! Please, Ivo!'

The call centre finally answered and she was forced to wait while he gave the details of the cards.

'Okay, all done. We'll get the new ones in a couple of days.'

'I don't want new cards. Ivo, promise me you won't go to the police!'

'Not this time.'

It was all she could ask for.

'Thank you.' She frowned. 'Then how…?'

'You're the sweet one in this partnership, I'm the cynical one. When I left this morning … Well, I didn't. I just parked around the corner and waited until your sister left, followed her back to the squat she's living in.'

'But that's…'

'Appalling?' He filled in the word for her. 'An invasion of privacy?'

She shook her head once, her thoughts a confused jumble of anger that he'd assumed her sister would steal from her. Gratitude that he'd had the foresight to take action. But then that was what Ivo did. He didn't wait for things to happen. He made them happen.

'No,' she managed. 'You were right.'

'I didn't do it because I thought she was going to steal from you, Belle. I did it so that you'd know where she was. In case she didn't come back.'

'Oh…' She was nearer to crying at that moment than she had been in years. He'd spent his morning hanging around, wasting time—something he never did—and he'd done it for her. 'Thank you.'

'Unless she's an experienced thief, she'll still have the stuff with her.'

'I can't believe…'

Won't was probably a better word, she thought. Didn't want to believe her sister was a thief. Only, perhaps, desperate…

'To be honest, neither do I,' Ivo said, taking her by surprise. 'I suspect it's a lot more complicated than that.'

'I'm not sure I can handle anything much more complicated.'

'I believe you can handle just about anything you set your mind to.' He regarded her steadily. 'I know you, Belle. You'd never give up on anything you really cared about.'

More question than statement, she thought. What was he asking?

'Can you lend me a little of that confidence?' she asked shakily.

'You don't need me, Belle. If I tell you where she is, you could handle it.'

Under his steady gaze she realised that it was true. That she'd faced the worst that could happen to her—leaving Ivo—and had survived.

She'd found the courage to walk away from a job that no longer interested her.

She'd shed a look that she'd outgrown.

'Maybe I could,' she said. 'But I'd like you to come with me.'

The squat was a five-storey Edwardian town house in the poor part of the area, boarded up, like its neighbours, waiting for the tide of gentrification to reach it.

Ivo had followed the girl on foot. She'd had her head down, barely looking up even when she'd crossed the road, only giving a cursory look around as she'd slipped round the back.

He'd held back then, giving her time to get under cover, before following her. It had been easy enough to pick out which house she was living in. A path had been worn across the overgrown backyard, half the board missing from an upstairs window.

He'd been prepared to step back, let Belle do this on her own, but he was relieved she'd asked him along. Was oddly grateful to Daisy for, unwittingly, bringing them together. For that alone, he'd do everything he could for the girl.

He led the way, testing the boards covering the rear door, the windows, until he found the loose one, slid it aside, climbed in.

'Maybe you should wait here,' he suggested as Belle made to follow him. Who knew what they'd find?

'I want to go to Daisy,' she said, climbing in after him. He didn't bother to argue. Instead he offered her his hand, pulling her up after him, steadying her as she dropped to the floor. 'Ugh! This is horrible.'

'Watch your step,' he warned as, hand still firmly grasping hers, he switched on the torch he'd brought from the car and shone it around the floor, checking for gaps. It looked sound enough, but looks could be deceptive. 'I don't imagine the boards are in that great a shape.'

'She can't stay here, Ivo!' Belle, responding to the dark, whispered. 'I can't leave her here. It's freezing. Damp. What *is* that smell?'

'Dry rot.' It was a smell the owner of every listed property dreaded. Then, 'You know if she wants to stay here there's nothing you can do about it.'

'You want to bet?'

'If we take this from her, she'll just move on somewhere else and we won't know where to find her.'

'According to you she'd come back.'

'Not now,' he said. Not now she'd stolen from her.

'We've got to do something,' she said. Then, almost reluctantly, 'She's pregnant, Ivo.'

There was something in her voice, something more than the loss of her sister—a transparent yearning that went straight to his gut.

'She told you that?' he asked, hoping that it was just another tug on vulnerable heartstrings. 'She looks anorexic to me.' She turned to stare at him and he realised he'd said too much. Well, she wasn't the only one with her emotions being ripped raw, exposed… 'Miranda,' he said, by way of explanation.

'Oh.' Then, as if everything had fallen into place, 'Oh.'

He'd never told her, had never shared that nightmare with her. It was his sister's secret, not his. Belle nodded as if it was all the explanation she needed. It wasn't. They'd started their marriage with a blank sheet. No baggage. That was the way he'd wanted it. But life wasn't like that. You were made by your family, your experiences.

You couldn't escape who you were.

'The nurse in the hospital told me that Daisy's pregnant,' Belle said, after a moment. 'That's why she passed out. She needs to be somewhere safe. She needs to be with me.'

'You asked her to stay?'

'Of course I did.' She shivered again. 'I've got to persuade her to come home with me, Ivo. Anything could happen to her here.'

'Don't worry. I'll issue an invitation that she won't be able to refuse.'

'What are you going to do?' Then, 'Not money!'

'Trust me, Belle. I won't repeat last night's mistake.' He tightened his grip on her hand. 'Come on.'

They picked their way across the rubbish-strewn floor, a safe path clearly marked by a passage in the dust made by wet footprints, leading upstairs.

Daisy had made one of the rooms at the back into a comfortable nest, using old furniture and bits of carpet scavenged from heaven alone knew where.

There was no electricity, but a little light filtered in through the filth on the window. Enough to see her sitting on the floor surrounded by credit cards, cash, the jewellery Belle had been wearing last night.

The wedding ring he'd placed on her finger.

She hadn't told him that Daisy had taken her ring, but he knew exactly when she'd discovered it was missing. That moment when she'd checked a drawer, clutched at her stomach as if in pain.

Pulling away from him, she reached for Daisy. 'Come home,' she said. 'Come home with me.'

'Go away.' Daisy pushed her away. 'I don't need you!'

'Please, Daisy. Let me take care of you. For your baby's sake.'

'I don't need you,' she repeated stubbornly. 'I don't want you.'

The words were vehement enough, but Ivo recognized the desperate need underlying Daisy's rejection. The girl had stolen from Belle, putting herself beyond her sister's love. If she was the one instigating rejection, then she remained in control.

He'd been through this when Miranda had been bent on the same course of self-destruction and knew how desperately hard it must be for Belle. It was hard for him to see her in so much pain.

'It's your choice,' he said, bending down to pick up one of the cards. 'You go with Belle, or you go with the police.'

He heard Belle's sharp intake of breath, but she caught his warning look, instantly understood what he was doing and said, 'I'm sorry, Daisy. You didn't just take my things. Some of the cards were issued on Ivo's accounts so I had to call him.'

'I didn't do anything with them,' she said sullenly, to him rather than Belle.

'Go home with Belle, now, and I'll forget it ever happened.'

She got to her feet, stuffed her hands in her pockets and headed for the door. Then, when they didn't follow, she stopped, looked back. 'What?'

He indicated the loot, scattered over the floor. 'Haven't you forgotten something?'

She stomped back, picked up the cards, the necklace, the earrings. Then began to search frantically. 'There was a ring. It was here. I know it was here.'

He felt almost proud of her. He'd expected her to brush over the fact that it wasn't there, deny she'd ever taken it. Maybe even believe she could come back and look for it later, if she needed a way out.

'I have it,' he said, opening his hand. And, taking Belle's left hand, he slipped it back on to her finger, holding it there for a moment. 'Maybe it's safer there.'

Belle felt the weight of the ring. Remembered the moment Ivo had placed it on her finger. How right it had felt, how happy she'd been. She tightened her hand as if she could recapture that precious memory.

'I won't lose it again,' she promised, her voice little more than a whisper. And for a moment it was as if they were back on that beach with a lifetime of possibilities ahead of them. Then, briskly, she turned away from him. You could never go back. 'Well,' she asked, 'what are we waiting for?'

'Don't you want these?' Daisy held out her hands, full of the things she'd picked up.

Belle glanced at them. 'Just stick it all in your pocket. We'll sort it all out when we get home.'

Ivo squeezed her hand, then released it. 'Come on, I'll take you home.'

'No...' Then, more firmly, 'No.' His approval meant a lot to her, but she wanted, needed to stand on her own feet. 'Daisy and I are going to walk home through the market.'

'Are you sure?'

Her wedding ring warmed against her finger. 'Quite sure. Thank you, Ivo.' Then she reached out, touched his arm. 'Call me.'

CHAPTER NINE

'WHERE is she today?'

Belle was saved from answering by the appearance of the waiter, bringing them water, taking their order.

'Daisy,' Ivo prompted, when he'd gone. Picking up as if they hadn't been interrupted. As if there was any other 'she'.

'I don't know,' she finally admitted. 'Don't look at me like that, Ivo…' frustrated, angry '…she was gone when I got home from the studio this morning.'

'Punishing you for putting work before her too?'

'She knows it's just until the end of the week.'

'Not like…' He stopped himself from saying the words. *Not like a marriage.* Then, 'She didn't leave a note?'

'She's an adult. She doesn't have to account for her time.' Then, a touch desperately, seeking reassurance. 'I have to trust her.'

He reached out, covered her hand with his own. 'I know. It's the hardest part.' He sat back, taking his hand with him. 'I'm not complaining. Having you to myself is more than I'd hoped for.'

Ivo had brought her a package that had been delivered to the Belgravia house, the first time in a week that he'd come to the flat, although, taking advantage of her invitation, he had called her every day just to chat. Ask how things were going. Supportive. Offering advice only when it was requested. There for her, but giving her space too. Giving her…respect.

But the truth was that she'd been going out of her mind with worry when she'd got home and Daisy wasn't there. Had practically fallen on his neck in gratitude when he'd suggested lunch. When he hadn't insisted on one of their usual fashionable haunts, the kind of place where everyone would know them, but agreed to her choice of this tiny Italian trattoria on the other side of Camden Market.

'How is it? Really?' he asked.

'Not easy,' she admitted. 'Apparently the adoption broke down after a couple of years and Daisy's been in more foster homes than she can count, then a halfway house. That's where she met this boy whose baby she's expecting.'

'Is he still in the picture?'

Belle shook her head. 'Daisy just wanted a baby.'

'He has the right to know.'

She looked up, surprised by the fierceness of Ivo's response. 'One step at a time, Ivo,' she said.

'Yes, of course. I'm sorry. I wasn't criticising. You're doing amazingly well.'

'Am I? The mood swings are difficult,' she admitted. 'She's up and down. Prickly one minute, loving the next.'

'Maybe it's her hormones.'

'It can't be helping. The doc's given her a clean bill of health at least and she's looking better. There's nothing wrong with her appetite.'

'So what's bothering you?'

She shook her head.

'There's something.'

'Nothing that can be solved with a new coat or a vitamin pill.' He waited. 'It's nothing at all. Stupid. She just hates that it's all one way. Seems to think she's a charity case. I can't get her to understand how much it means to me to be able to do stuff for her.'

'She thinks you're going to lose interest. That she daren't care too much in case you dump her like everyone else in her life.'

'But that's…' About to say ridiculous, she realised that it wasn't. That somehow Ivo knew exactly how Daisy was feeling. She realised just how little she knew about his past beyond the privileged lifestyle, the fact that his parents had been killed just after he'd graduated. 'If I didn't know better, I'd think you'd read Psychology at Uni, instead of Economics. How come you understand her better than I do?'

'You're doing fine.'

An evasion.

'Maybe what she needs is a job. Something to make her feel useful. Give her something of her own so that her entire life isn't invested in you.'

'Or make her think I'm getting ready to pitch her back out into the big wide world. Especially if she thinks the idea has come from you.'

'She thinks I'm some kind of threat to her?'

Ivo sensed rather than heard Belle's sigh and it provoked mixed feelings. The fact that Belle was still wearing her wedding ring had given him hope. And if Daisy sensed a threat, then it meant that Belle talked about him.

'She's fragile, Ivo. Needs to be the sole focus of attention.'

She didn't have to tell him. He knew how needy, how self-centered, how destructive the damaged psyche could be.

'Maybe it would be better if I left Manda to suggest it.'

'Manda!'

He smiled at her horrified response. 'Trust me. She knows what she's doing.'

He understood her lack of enthusiasm; Manda had given her a hard time, he knew. 'Really,' he assured her. 'In fact, I suspect you have a new fan.'

'Now I'm really worried. What exactly have you told her, Ivo?'

'Just enough, so that when this hits the headlines she'll be prepared to be door-stepped by the press.' He glanced at her. 'Any news from your Aussie friend?' She shook her head. 'It's like waiting for the other shoe to drop, isn't it?'

'A bit.' She regarded him curiously. 'You're good at this, aren't you?'

'It's easier for me. My responses aren't muddied by emotion.'

About to say that was because he didn't do 'emotion' she stopped herself. She was beginning to suspect that it wasn't a lack of emotion that kept him buttoned up, but a fear of letting it spill out.

'It's more than that, Ivo. You seem to know just what Daisy's feeling.'

'I have a sister.'

'That's it?' On the point of laughing at the idea of Miranda being an angsty teen, she thought better of it. Ivo had told her a little of what his sister had been through. 'I'm trying to focus on the early days with Daisy. It's when we were together,' she explained. 'A family.'

'You don't blame her, do you? Your mother?'

'She was trying to protect us,' she said. 'And she was my mum. Unconditional love is a parent/child thing.'

Something she'd longed for too. Something a child would have given her. That she'd believed her sister, in her new home, would be able to give, to receive—something precious that would blot out everything else.

'Daisy's father was a gambler, Ivo. He ran up debts, mortgaged my mother's house with three different companies, borrowed money from loan sharks and then disappeared. Mum never saw the letters from the bank or the finance people. I imagine he'd lain in wait for the postman and siphoned them off. The first she knew anything was wrong was when the bailiffs turned up.'

'That's fraud. He could have gone to prison.'

'Yes, well, first you had to catch him. Then you had to prove that he'd done it. All academic, because a couple of loan shark heavies threatened Daisy, held a knife to her throat until my mother handed over her child allowance, issued an instruction to be there every Monday morning for a repeat performance.'

He swore, something he did so rarely that Belle's eyes widened in shock. 'Why didn't she go to the police?' he demanded.

'The graphic description of what would happen to both her children if she did?'

He let slip another expletive, betraying just how deeply affected he was. 'I'm sorry…'

'No, that describes him perfectly. Mum got us home, packed what she could carry and ran.'

'Four years? You lived like that for four years?'

'Something inside her broke, Ivo. My dad was supposed to be the bad one. He drank, he knocked her about, fell into the canal one night—or was pushed—and drowned. Daisy's dad looked and acted like a gentleman. She thought the sun shone out of his eyes. He told her he was going away on business for a few days and while she was ironing and packing for him, he was emptying her purse. When her world fell apart, she wasn't capable of putting her life back together. There were people who could have helped; she was just too broken to see it.'

'And still Daisy wants to find this man? Acknowledge him as her father?'

'Unconditional love,' she repeated. 'It's given to bad parents as well as good ones.'

'Not always,' he said. 'Not if you don't know what love is. Not if you've never known it.'

Ivo knew that to compare the misery of his childhood with what she'd been through was beyond pathetic. But she'd bared her soul to him. Had told him things that she hadn't told anyone. She deserved as much from him. The truth; the whole truth. Because, like her, he'd lived a lie, had hidden behind a façade of the perfect life. The man who had everything, including the country's sweetheart, Belle Davenport. Except that had all been a lie too.

Well, he was done with lies. Belle had been brave enough to confront her past; he could do no less. And if anyone was capable of understanding, it was Belle.

'My parents didn't love each other and they sure as hell didn't love us.'

Belle was frowning, clearly confused. 'But I thought…you had everything. The wonderful holidays in France, Italy. I've heard you and Miranda talk about them.'

'Did you ever hear either of us mention our parents?'

She thought about it. 'Well, no.' She sat back. 'No, I suppose not.'

'We barely knew them. Neither of them wanted to be bothered

with us, even with a nanny to do the dirty work. We were shunted off to boarding school at the earliest possible age. Learned behaviour. Our grandparents were no different. Forget seen but not heard. We weren't even wanted for decoration.'

'I had no idea.'

'No, well, maybe we both had stuff we didn't want to talk about, Belle. Didn't want to remember.'

'Only the holidays. Who did you spend them with?'

'Every year we were dumped with some family who took in kids for the summer while they went off on their own affairs. And I do mean affairs. We were just getting to the age when we might have been interesting enough for them to notice when they were drowned. What they were doing on the same yacht has always been something of a mystery to me.'

'I'm so sorry.'

'Don't be. And some of the families were wonderful. Some summers. Those are the ones we remember, talk about.'

'And the rest?'

'We survived until a universal aunt arrived to take us back to school.'

'And you hated that too?'

'Hate would be too strong a word. It was just all a bit unrelenting. There was never any warmth. No one to give you a hug.'

He realised he was gripping her hand, clinging on to it as if to stop himself from drowning. He forced himself to release it but, before he could lift it away, she caught it, held it, then pushed her chair back.

He rose automatically as she got to her feet, held his breath as she came round the table. 'No…' The word, wrenched from him as she put her arms around him, pulled him close, was scarcely audible.

She was soft, warm, against him. He'd tried so hard not to admit to feelings that he knew would break him. Had built a barrier to protect himself. Had not allowed himself to get too close because he knew that one day she would give up waiting for what he could not give her.

Himself. A child…

And with one hug she had brought the whole edifice tumbling down so that he clung to her, held her, felt something that could only be tears stinging his eyes.

Belle leaned back, looked at him, then reached up, wiped her fingers over his cheek. 'Let's go home, Ivo,' she said softly.

Her scent filled him like a warm balm to the spirit and the temptation to accept the comfort that she was offering was almost beyond enduring. The only thing that would be worse would be the aftermath.

'I can't.'

He was scarcely able to believe he'd said the words. This was what he'd wanted. Her back in his arms, warming the ice. But he couldn't do it to her. Not again. He thought he'd loved her too much to let her go. Now he understand the difference between need and love. He'd seen real love in action. It wasn't about need, about self; it was about giving, about sacrifice, about doing what was best for the person you cared for.

'I can't,' he repeated.

He lowered her into her chair, carefully placed himself on the far side of the table, tried to blot out that confused look of rejection confronting him, a look that he knew from the inside.

'I thought I could,' he said. 'I thought I had it all worked out. You were restless. You'd been thrown out of the groove by your Himalayan trip and you were tired of what you were doing. I thought all I had to do was stick around, point you in the direction of something that would grab your attention, distract you from the emptiness in our lives—'

'Ivo…'

'No. Don't stop me, Belle. I have to say this. Have to tell you the truth.'

She made as if to say something, swallowed, waited, her face set and white.

The waiter arrived with a platter of antipasto. Did something fancy with a pepper mill. Finally left them alone.

They shouldn't be here, he thought. They should be somewhere quiet. Somewhere private. And yet maybe this was best. A public place where emotion had to be kept on a tight rein.

'I thought—believed,' he said, carrying on as if they had not been interrupted, 'that if you found something new to fill your life, then you'd be able to forget, that a moment would come when you'd slip back into your place in my life and then everything would be as it should be. Ordered. Tidy.'

'Forget what, Ivo?'

'That you'd made a bad deal. That security without love, without a family, without…without children, was never going to be enough for someone like you. I wanted you so much…' He closed his ears to her gasp of something very like pain, forced himself to continue. 'Needed you. Beyond reason. Maybe, if I'd known, understood that you wanted more, needed more, I would have found the strength to walk away.' He would have been abandoning all that was vital, alive in him, but he'd have been in control. 'I believed you when you said you only wanted the security of marriage. None of the emotional trappings. Or maybe I was grasping at straws, desperate to believe you because that way I didn't have to address my conscience. Tell you the truth.'

'What truth?' A tiny crease furrowed the space between her eyes. 'Tell me, Ivo.'

'In those few precious days we spent together after the wedding, you began talking about the future as if it was real. About having children.' He looked up, faced her. 'I can't go home with you, Belle. I can't be the husband you need—you deserve. I know, I've always known, that I can never give you children.'

He saw the confusion, the frown deepen as she struggled to comprehend the magnitude of what he had told her.

'Is that…' She stopped. 'Is that why we came home from our honeymoon early?' She struggled to say more. 'Is that why you chose to sleep separately? Because you thought I wouldn't stay. If I knew.'

He nodded, just once. 'I should have told you.'

'Yes, you should. But then we should have told one another a lot of things, Ivo, but if I'd married you simply for children, I wouldn't have stayed after I saw…' She was struggling with the words. Paused to gather herself. 'I couldn't have stayed when you left me alone on the pretext of flying off to deal with some business crisis.'

'How did you know?'

'That it was a lie? You didn't have to say anything, Ivo. You're good at hiding your feelings, but that day I could read you like a book. I knew that you didn't love me, that I was always going to be a temporary wife, but when we were alone, after the wedding, I glimpsed a sight of some fairy tale happy ever after. Made the mistake of sharing it. One look at your face told me I was on my own…'

'So why didn't you leave then?' He dragged a hand over his face, struggling to understand what she was telling him.

Belle swallowed. She'd got it so wrong. Right from the beginning she should have fought for her marriage. Fought to hold on to something precious. She'd been so afraid to show him how she felt. Overwhelmed by that horrible house. Intimidated by his sister…

'I was afraid,' she said. 'Afraid I'd lose you.'

'Then, why now?'

She looked at him. She'd been so afraid, but she wasn't now. She was struggling, but she was winning—a new life, a sister. Maybe, if she was brave enough, she could even have the marriage she'd always wanted.

'I left because I hated myself for compromising. For hoping and hoping that one day you'd wake up and…' she made a helpless gesture as if the words were too difficult '…*see* me. Be the man I'd glimpsed on our honeymoon. Relaxed, happy…'

'They were the happiest days I've ever spent.'

'Then why? Why couldn't you talk to me?'

'You were not the only one who was afraid. You were the most beautiful woman I'd ever met. No!' he said, when her dismissive gesture suggested that she'd made her point.

That she was no more than a temporary trophy wife.

'I'm not talking about your looks, although that's true too. You are lovely. It was your warmth, your vitality, a smile that could melt permafrost that drew me to you. I always knew you wouldn't stay.'

'Permafrost? You appear to have overestimated its power.'

'No. If you hadn't melted it, why would I care?'

'I didn't leave you because you so plainly didn't want children, Ivo. I left you because I couldn't stand the coldness. The distance. Couldn't bear the thought of waking up alone one more day.' And then, as if everything had suddenly fallen into place. 'That's what you've been doing, isn't it?'

He didn't ask her what she was talking about. In the last week he'd talked to her about Daisy. And about Miranda.

His sister's desperate need for love had driven her into a series of disastrous relationships. Too needy, too desperate. When, over and over again, everyone she loved, in whom she had invested her emotions, rejected her, she'd spiralled down into a destructive phase of anorexia. Rejecting herself.

Stealing from Belle, he knew, had been prompted by the same self-destruct response in Daisy. Anticipating rejection, she'd provoked it.

He'd been there himself. Had fought his own demons in his own way. Self-destruction came with the territory.

'You were waiting for me to reject you,' Belle said, slowly, wonderingly. 'Protecting yourself from being hurt.'

'It didn't work.'

'You held me at such a distance, Ivo—'

'I meant about the hurt.' Living with himself had been a world of hurt. The only relief had been in her arms and selfishly he'd sought to win her back. Keep her. 'I cheated you. Lied to you. You were right to leave. You deserve better.'

'Life isn't about what we deserve, Ivo.' She raised her hands in a helpless gesture. 'If it was about what we deserved then there wouldn't be any kids on their own, cold and hungry. Scared women. Men for whom fatherhood is an unfulfilled dream.'

'Leave me out of your list of deserving souls.'

'Why? You've suffered too.' Then, with a sudden frown, 'What happened to you, Ivo?' she demanded, the bit between her teeth now, fearless in her refusal to accept anything less than the whole truth. 'Were you sick as a child? How do you know that you can't have children?'

He'd hoped she wouldn't think to ask him that. Unlikely. What man, unless he'd attempted to father a child and failed, would know he was infertile?

He had none of the pity-inducing excuses to offer. No mumps or childhood fever to blame. Only himself.

'I know,' he said, 'because ten years ago I had a vasectomy.'

A vasectomy.

The word filled her head, swelling until she thought it would explode.

Belle looked at the food laid out temptingly on a platter for them to help themselves. Grilled baby aubergines, olives, sun-dried tomatoes, paper thin slices of meat. All of them untouched.

She made a helpless gesture, then, covering her hand with her mouth to hold in the cry of pain, she scrambled to her feet, rushed outside, desperate for air.

Just desperate.

Neither of them said a word when Ivo emerged in a rush a few moments later, catching up with her as she walked blindly through the lunchtime crowds of the market, draping her abandoned coat around her shoulders.

The tenderness of the gesture caught her unawares. Without warning, the strength went out of her legs and she subsided on to a bench, sat, bent double, her face pressed against her knees.

The awful thing was that she didn't have to ask why he'd done it. She knew. Understood. The sins of the father. His grandparents, his parents, the fear that he too would follow the genetic imprint—become another cold, distant parent of unhappy children.

Understood why he was so driven—the relentless pursuit of wealth and power filling a bottomless void.

He sat beside her, not touching her, said, as much to himself as to her, 'At the time it seemed so rational.'

She didn't look up, just reached out a hand. There was an endless space of time before his fingers made contact with hers;

maybe he thought that she was the one who needed comfort. He wasn't a man who knew how to ask for it.

'I suspect I was on the edge of a breakdown. Miranda was already there. I'd just signed the papers to keep her in hospital for her own protection…'

'You don't have to explain.' She risked an attempt to sit up. The world tilted, then steadied. 'Really,' she said, 'I understand.'

'Do you?'

Oh, yes. He'd thought he was protecting some unborn child from what he'd been through. He was, like Miranda, like her sister, like her when she'd been too scared to tell him that she was marrying him not because of his millions, but because she couldn't imagine living without him—like most people faced with the prospect of pain—just doing what he had to in order to protect himself.

Not self-destruction, but self-preservation.

'I tried to have it reversed. When I realised what I'd done. What I'd done to you.'

She turned to look at him then. 'You'd have done that for me?'

'I…' He faltered. 'Yes, I'd have done that. Done anything.'

'Except say the words.'

'I…I didn't know how to.'

'There is more than one way of showing love, Ivo. Words are the least of them.'

The fact was he hadn't left her on their honeymoon, left her to return home and face Miranda's cold welcome by herself simply to chase down some deal, but to try and have the vasectomy reversed.

'I'd been able to justify what I'd done, marrying you, not telling you, because…' He broke off.

'Because I said that the only reason I'd marry you, marry anyone was for security.'

'Sex and money. I thought we'd both got what we wanted and then you started talking about a future, a real future, children, and I knew—'

She tightened her grip on his hand to stop him.

'—I knew that's what I wanted too,' he persisted. 'I'd just been too afraid to admit it to you, to myself. I thought I could fix it. That I could come back and we could begin again. But you didn't wait.'

No. He'd said he would come back once he'd dealt with 'business' but there had seemed no point. They had been in paradise and she had wanted more. Had destroyed it.

'Don't,' she said. 'Please don't blame yourself. Neither of us were brave enough to risk everything for something as dangerous as love.'

'No.' Then again, 'No.' And, almost to himself, '"…*the coward does it with a kiss*…"' He sighed. 'Confronted with what I'd done to you, I knew I had to get home to see the doctor who'd performed the original surgery. Beg him for a miracle.'

'I'm so sorry…'

He shook his head, rejecting her pity. Never had she felt so helpless. Felt the lack of words to express the way she ached for him.

'I can't say I wasn't warned when I first went to him. He hadn't wanted to do it. Had advised me against it, suggested some kind of counselling. He only relented when I made it clear that if he wouldn't do it there and then, I'd find someone who would, even if it meant going abroad. He was kind enough not to remind me of that.'

He looked down at their locked hands.

'When I thought Daisy was your daughter, when I thought that you had a chance to be a mother, it seemed like a gift. The miracle I'd hoped for.'

'A difficult teenager?' She managed a smile. 'Not everyone's idea of a miracle.'

'She'd have been *your* difficult teenager. Our difficult teenager,' he said, and she thought her heart would break for him. Almost wished she had been a teenage mum with a kid out there somewhere just waiting for her to get in touch.

'She's not my daughter, Ivo, but she still needs us. If it hadn't been for you…' She looked at him. 'Did I ever say thank you for what you did?'

'Don't…' He shook his head. 'Don't ever thank me.'

She owed him more than thanks, but she let it go and said, 'Daisy needs us, Ivo. Not just me, but you. A decent man in her life. And there's her baby. Seven months from now there'll be a little one who'll need an aunt and uncle to spoil him or her rotten.'

'Don't be kind, Belle. Don't pretend that it doesn't matter. I saw your face when you told me that Daisy is expecting a baby.'

'Still jealous of my little sister? Not a very attractive picture, is it? Especially from someone as lucky as I've been.'

'Luck had nothing to do with it. You radiate warmth, Belle. It was there from the first moment you looked up from the telethon switchboard, smiled into the camera, said "Call me" in that sweet, sexy voice. Half the country reached for their phones.'

'Sex sells,' she said dismissively. 'I got my break because it was hot and I'd undone one too many buttons.'

'Do you really think that's why the network is so desperate to hang on to you that they'd pay you any amount of money? Because of your cleavage?' He finally smiled. 'Lovely though it is.'

'No. They're offering me big money because it's easier—cheaper—than finding someone to take my place. Go through all the time-consuming, expensive, image-building hoops with someone new.'

He breathed out another uncharacteristic expletive and said, 'You haven't got an egotistical bone in your body, have you?'

'What have I got to be vain about? Other people put me together, made me what I am.'

'You really don't get it, do you?' he said, not bothering to hide the fact that he was angry with her.

'Ivo…' she protested uncertainly. He didn't lose his temper, didn't get angry.

'What you are, Belle, what makes you a star, won you that award, has nothing to do with image consultants or PR. The viewers adored you from that first husky giggle, a fact the network wasted no time in taking advantage of. All the professionals did was put the polish on a very rare diamond.'

'Oh, please!' Belle knew she was blushing. It was ridicu-

lous... Then, 'I have to get back,' she said. 'Daisy will be won-
dering where I am.'

'You're an adult, Belle,' he replied, refusing to back off.
'Daisy has to learn to trust you when you're out on a date.'

And without warning the whole tenor of the conversation
shifted. One moment he'd been angry with her, the next his eyes
were a soft hazy blue-grey that she knew was for her alone. That
never failed to stir an echo from somewhere deep inside her.

She swallowed. 'This is a date?'

'We're sitting on a bench holding hands. The last time we
did that...'

He stopped, but her memory filled in the rest. The last time
had been the first time. She'd been talking to someone about the
charity they were all supporting that night when something had
made her turn. It was all the invitation he'd needed and a path
had seemed to open up before him as he'd walked across the
Serpentine Gallery, offered her his hand and said, 'Ivo Grenville.'

And she'd said, 'Belle Davenport.' And took it.

And that was all. He was a workaholic millionaire, she was a
television celebrity, their histories were public knowledge and
words weren't necessary. And when she placed her hand in his,
he tucked it beneath his arm and walked out of the gallery with
her, through the dusky park, along the side of the lake until,
eventually, they'd reached a bench set in the perfect spot. And
they'd sat on it, her arm tucked beneath his, his hand holding hers.

'I remember,' she said, her voice thick with regret for all the
wasted years. Was it too late? Could they go back to that moment? Start again? 'Do you remember what comes next?'

Around them the market was a blur of noise and colour but
Ivo was back in another time—another place; in the warmth, the
stillness of a summer's evening with a beautiful woman who, like
him, had recognised the moment for what it was. For whom
words were an irrelevance.

'Do you remember?' she asked again.

Ivo rubbed his thumb over the ring he'd placed on her finger.
He remembered. Every touch, every look. Eyes like warm but-

terscotch, hair gleaming pale as silver, a soft, inviting mouth waiting for him to take a step outside the emotional vacuum in which he'd imprisoned himself. Waiting now, for him to find the courage to finally break free.

He stood up, his hand beneath hers inviting her to do the same. She rose at his touch, waited.

He lifted a hand to her hair, as he had then.

'Did I tell you that I like this new style?' he said. 'That you look wonderful?'

She didn't answer, seeming to know that he was talking to himself rather than her.

He laid his palm against her cheek and she leaned into it, nestling against his hand, closing her eyes.

'Look at me,' he said.

And when she raised her head, lifted heavy lashes, he kissed her—no more than the touching of lips, it was deeper, more meaningful than any exchanged in hot passion. It said, as it had said then, everything he could never put into words. Say out loud. Admit to.

'You remembered,' she said, her sweet mouth widening into a smile.

'How could I ever forget?'

A kiss. A cab ride. The slow sensual dance of a man and woman making love for the first time. Each touch something rare and new. Each kiss a promise.

'You took me home,' she said, tucking her arm beneath his and turning to walk the short distance to her flat. 'And stayed to be dragged out of sleep by my four o'clock alarm call.'

'I remember.' Then, 'That's not why—'

'I know,' she said quickly. 'I understand now why you wanted separate rooms. Why you left my bed.'

'Because the kiss was a lie. If I'd loved you, truly loved you, I'd have walked away then.'

Instead he'd deceived her. Deceived himself. Fooling himself that he was taking no more than the minimum.

Protecting himself from the moment when she'd see their

marriage for what it was—a hollow sham. And then, when she'd done just that, driven away by his coldness, he'd discovered that there was no way of protecting himself from loving Belle Davenport. That he couldn't live without her.

'Don't be so hard on yourself, Ivo.'

'Why not?'

She didn't answer, but as they reached her front door, she handed him the keys and he unlocked it, remained on the step. She didn't take them from him, but walked up the stairs, leaving him with no choice but to follow.

She'd already tapped on the flat door by the time he joined her. 'No answer. Daisy's still out,' she said, standing back so that he could open that door too, dropping her bag on the hall table before sliding her hands around his neck.

'Belle…'

He'd said her name in just that way too, that first time. Then it had been a warning that once he'd stepped over the threshold there would be no turning back. Now it was more complex.

He wanted her and right at this moment he was sure she wanted him, but it was simple need, comfort they both craved. Afterwards, nothing would have changed.

'I can't,' he said. 'It wouldn't be right.'

'Just lie with me, Ivo. Hold me.' And, for the first time since he'd known her, the tears that brimmed in her eyes spilled over and ran, unchecked, down her cheeks. 'Please. I'm so tired. I can't sleep. But if you held me, just for a little while…'

Denying her was beyond him and he took her coat from her shoulders, hung it, alongside his own, on the stand, then took her hand and led her to her bedroom, undressing her slowly, as he had time without number, each button, hook, zip, each brush of his fingers against warm skin sweet torture. When she was naked, utterly defenceless, he lifted back the soft down quilt, settled her beneath it. Then he, understanding her need for closeness, began to undress.

This was new.

This was new, different, important beyond imagining.

For the first time in three years he was about to share a bed with his wife and not make love to her.

Or maybe he was. Because that was what this was, he thought as he slid in beside her, put his arms around her and pulled her back against him, fitting her to his body like a spoon. Gently kissed her shoulder, whispering soft words of reassurance, words of love that spilled out of some locker where they'd been stored away, not needed in this life.

This was the love, comfort, sharing, being there for someone that he'd been running from all his adult life. He nestled his face into the back of her neck, breathed in her familiar scent. Vanilla. Rose. Something darker, more potent that stirred the passions.

He'd imagined having to fight down his body's aching need for her, do quadratic equations in his head to distract himself, but it wasn't like that. This wasn't about him; it was about Belle. Giving back all he'd taken.

And conversely feeding his desire on a completely different level, transcending the purely physical; this closeness, just holding her, met his needs, fulfilled them in every way that mattered. And he closed his eyes.

CHAPTER TEN

BELLE stirred, turned over and found that she was still lying in Ivo's arms. She'd slept—not surprising; she rose at four every morning to go to the studio.

But it wasn't her brief nap that made her feel brand-new. It was Ivo, holding her, being there.

She'd slept and he hadn't left her.

All her dreams rolled into one. Or as near as they could be and she grinned, madly, stupidly happy.

'This brings a whole new meaning to the expression "they slept together",' she said.

Then, because this felt like the start of something new, something different, rather than an ending, she reached out to lay her hand against his heart.

He caught her wrist, held her an inch away from his skin.

'Belle…'

She ignored the warning. He believed she wanted more than he could give her and because of that had kept her at a distance. Kept himself at a distance.

He was wrong.

Now she knew the truth a world of possibilities opened up before them. Before her. There were countless children for whom she could make a difference, with her time, her love, her money. There was only one man. And with one arm trapped beneath her, one hand occupied keeping hers captive, he was at her mercy.

With her hand neutralised she did what any woman would do and used her mouth to break down his resistance.

She heard the hiss of agony as she laid her lips against his heart, feeling the hammer of it. His skin was warm, like silk beneath her tongue.

He tried to speak, caught his breath as she curled her tongue around his nipple, tasting him, savouring him as it responded, tightening to her touch. The power was all hers and she used it, taking her mouth across his chest to the concave space beneath his ribs. He gathered himself then, made an effort to put an end to this raid on his senses, but he'd left it too late and the soft twirl of her tongue around his navel wrung a groan, more pain than pleasure, from him.

He was a strong-minded man, but his body betrayed him, rising to meet her. She welcomed it with open mouth.

Ivo had swiftly discovered that quadratic equations were no match for his wife when she was set upon seduction. That when he should have been saying 'No…', the only word he seemed capable of saying was 'Yes…' That when she straddled him, leaned forward so that her luscious breasts stroked against his chest, sheathed herself on him, as she said, 'I love you. Love me, Ivo…' that the small warning voice hammering away somewhere inside his head was wasting its time.

Afterwards, when they'd made love with no secrets, no barriers between them, she cried. He wrapped his arms around her and held her close.

'I'm sorry,' she said, dashing her tears away with the back of her hand. 'I don't do this…' Then, smiling, if somewhat shakily, 'You didn't bargain on this when you dropped by with that package, did you?'

'I might start sending them to you myself if this is the welcome I get,' he said. Then, 'Or you could just come home.'

She stiffened. 'I can't. I can't go back there…' Then, 'Did you hear something?'

A crash, then the sound of the front door being slammed, the feet pounding down the stairs, made denial impossible and Belle catapulted out of his arms, grabbed a dressing gown, clutching it around herself as she wrenched open the door.

'Oh…'

She sounded as if she'd been punched, as if the air had been driven from her and he didn't stop to pull on his pants, but followed, coming to an abrupt halt in the doorway of the small third bedroom that Belle had converted to a wardrobe and dressing room.

The dress that she'd worn for the awards ceremony, the lace evening coat, had been reduced to litter. Mere shreds of material.

Daisy.

How long must it have taken her? How long had she been home? Seeing his coat hanging beside Belle's, the shut bedroom door, standing there, listening to the sounds made by two people lost to the world as they made love.

He looked up and saw that the scissors she'd used had been flung at the mirror.

His instinct was to reach for Belle, protect her from this, but she twitched away from him, rejecting a gesture of comfort that an hour before she'd begged for, the kind of gesture that was fast becoming second nature to him.

'Something's happened,' she said. 'Something bad.' She turned on him. 'She needed me, Ivo, and I wasn't there for her.'

He drew in a breath, hunting for something to say, anything to help reassure her. To reassure himself. The painful reality was that sometimes there were no words.

'She'll have gone to the squat.'

'Why would she do that? She knows it's the first place I'll look for her.'

He wondered if the switch from 'we' to 'I' was conscious, or whether Belle had slipped instinctively into self-preservation mode in anticipation of what was to come, already anticipating the worst.

'She wants you to find her, Belle.' He indicated the coat stand where she'd hung the expensive quilted jacket that her sister had bought her alongside his overcoat. 'She didn't take a coat.'

Because she wanted to punish her sister, but he kept his thoughts to himself.

'She'll be freezing.'

'Come on, I'll drive you—'

'No!' Then, more firmly, 'No.'

Daisy had helped to bring them closer, to open up, let light and air into the dark core of suffering that they'd chosen to bury, but she was a loose cannon and, in her need, was just as capable of driving them apart.

Forced to choose between them—and Daisy would make her choose—Belle, driven by guilt, would sacrifice anything to convince her sister that she was loved. Him. Her own happiness.

All he could do was hang in there. Do whatever he could to make it easy for her. Starting now.

'She'll want to shout at someone. Blame someone for the fact that when she needed you, you were in bed with me. If I'm there she can use me as her verbal punch bag,' he said.

'I wanted you, Ivo. This isn't your fault.'

'This isn't about us. She needs you, Belle. I'm dispensable.'

The squat had been secured against intruders—he'd called the property developers himself to make sure it was done quickly and they'd made a solid job of it.

Daisy had clearly tried to kick her way in—there were footprints on the new board—but, beaten, she was now sitting, hunched up, shivering, her hands stuffed into her sleeves, on a low wall.

Belle said nothing, just handed her the coat she'd left behind and was invited, in the most basic of terms, to go away. Her response was to take off her own coat, lay the two of them side by side on the wall and sit down beside her.

'Do you want to tell me what happened?' she asked matter-of-factly.

'Like you care.'

'If I didn't care I wouldn't be here. What happened?' she repeated quietly.

'You *weren't* there!'

Daisy sounded more like a petulant child than a grown woman, Ivo thought, but she'd been through a lot. Would need

a great deal of help, counselling, endless amounts of that unconditional love that Belle talked about, to build up her self-esteem.
He knew from experience that it was a full-time job.

'When wasn't I there?' Belle asked patiently.

'This morning when the agency phoned.'

'I was at work, Daisy. You know that.' Calm, steady. He knew
how hard that was and he was desperately proud of her. 'What
did they want?'

'They found my dad.'

'What?'

Belle, doing her best to remain calm, composed, controlled,
was shaken to her foundations and Daisy finally looked at her.

'They called this morning to tell me that they'd found him.'

'But they shouldn't have…' She'd given express instructions
to the agency.

'What? Told me? Why? He was *my* dad.'

'I know, but… I wanted to be there when they talked to you.
You shouldn't have been on your own.'

'It's nothing new.'

'That was then. This is now.'

'Right.' Disbelief. A glance in Ivo's direction that said it all.
'I can't believe they told you. Wait until—'

'They thought I was you. One Miss Porter is pretty much like
another on the telephone. They had news; I wasn't going to say
call back when my big sister's home, was I?' And, without
warning, her face crumpled. 'He's dead, Bella. My dad died six
months ago. I went to see his grave. I took flowers. It was horrible. There was no headstone. No name. Just a number.'

'Oh, darling,' Belle said, putting her arms around her. 'You
shouldn't have been alone.' And she never would be again. This
afternoon she'd seen a different Ivo—someone caring, someone
capable of immense feeling, the man she'd glimpsed in those first
heady days, the man she'd fallen in love with and she'd wanted
him, had pushed him into something he knew was a mistake.
Selfish, selfish, selfish… 'I'm so sorry.'

'Oh, please!' She shook her off. 'You don't care. You hated

him, blamed him for everything.' Belle, Ivo could see, was struggling to find a response that wasn't going to curdle in her mouth, something to comfort Daisy, but her sister didn't wait. 'You hated him and you don't give a damn about me.' She looked up, glared at him over Belle's shoulder and said, 'He's the only person you ever think about.'

'No…'

'It's true. He's always calling you. When you talk to him your face goes all soft and gooey and when I came home he was there, in your room. I heard you! You're supposed to be separated, getting a divorce, not having sex in the middle of the afternoon!'

Her youthful outrage would have been funny, Ivo thought, but he felt no urge to laugh. Belle's desperate 'No…' had chilled him to the bone. He'd known it would be bad—the destruction of the dress was not the work of a girl mildly irritated with her sister— but this was worse than he could ever have imagined.

And when Belle turned and looked at him, he knew he was right. Knew that she would sacrifice her own happiness, this tender shoot that promised a new beginning to their marriage— anything to make up to her sister for a mistake she'd made when she was fourteen years old. A decision she'd made for the best of reasons. The truth was that Daisy needed one hundred per cent of her sister right now and that was what she'd get.

There was nothing he could do or say to change Belle's mind. That to even try would be to hurt her more than she was already hurting.

He knew because he'd have done the same for Miranda. Would have sacrificed anything to make her well, make her whole; but her words, as she continued to look at him, still tore his heart from his body.

'Today was just one of those things that sometimes happens when something important is over, Daisy. Revisiting the might-have-beens. The very-nearlys. But we can never go back.'

Her words were telling him that waiting was not an option, that she had made her decision, that today had meant nothing. But her eyes, begging him to understand, to forgive her for putting Daisy first, were saying something else and, as if she knew that they betrayed her, she closed them, turned away, drew Daisy close as if she were a child.

'You're more important to me than anyone in the world, Daisy Porter. No one can ever come between us. You have to believe that.'

There were tears in her eyes as she said it, but Daisy, sobbing out her own grief, for a man she'd never known, who'd never loved her, who'd robbed them both of the life they should have had, didn't see them.

Life had a way of calling you on bad decisions, Ivo knew. He hadn't walked away three years ago, hadn't had Belle's heart, her capacity for sacrifice. This time, though, things were different. Belle had taught him the power of love, its enduring nature.

She needed this time alone with her sister and he was strong enough to give her the space she needed, for as long as she needed.

'For as long as we both shall live.'

He repeated the words from the marriage service under his breath, the difference being that this time he understood what they meant. And, more importantly, he believed them.

'You should have an early night,' Belle said.

Daisy had her feet up on the sofa she'd chosen—fuchsia-pink velvet, not as practical, but a lot more exciting than the brown suede she'd picked out—watching television.

'An early night?' She'd got over her tears, had a bath and a slice of pizza, which was all she seemed to want to eat. 'I'm not a kid.'

Then stop acting like one, she wanted to yell at her. Grow up. I had to. Ivo had to…

She held it in. This was her fault. If she'd been there, if she'd fought with the social workers for access, visiting rights, maybe it would have all worked out.

If she hadn't lost all sense today, hadn't been thinking solely of herself, then maybe, gradually, she could have slowly built on this brand-new fledgling relationship with Ivo.

Instead Daisy, selfish, needy, desperate, had forced her to

choose between her sister and her marriage. She didn't know that she'd already chosen Daisy when she'd left Ivo.

For a moment she'd believed that he could be a part of their lives. But he understood the problems, the sacrifice involved in taking care of someone who had been emotionally damaged, broken by circumstance.

There had been no need for words. He'd made it easy for her, making it clear, when he'd dropped them back at the flat that he wouldn't be around for a while. Offering some excuse about pressure of business…

She dragged her mind back to her life, said, 'I didn't say you were a kid, but it's my last day on the breakfast sofa tomorrow, Daisy. I'd like you to be there with me.'

'What?' For a moment she looked excited, then just plain scared. 'Oh, no…' Then she bounced back. 'My hair!'

'The make-up girls will fix it for you.'

'But what will I wear? Can I borrow your…?' she began. Then, as quickly as it had bubbled up, her excitement evaporated and she sank back into the sofa. 'Forget it. You don't want me there.'

'I wouldn't have asked if I didn't want you there. I want the world to know I have a sister.'

'Parade me as your charity case? No thanks.'

She was doing it deliberately. For a moment she'd forgotten about the dress. What she'd done to it.

'You don't have to punish yourself over the dress, Daisy,' she said. 'You did it. It happened. You apologised. Now move on.' She didn't move. 'Okay. Let's deal with this. Come on.'

'What?' But Belle had her by the hand and, before she knew what was happening, they were in the room where all her gowns were hanging on rails, waiting for a carpenter to find time to start work on fitted wardrobes.

Nothing had been touched since Daisy's attack on her dress. She'd simply shut the door on it, unable to face what it meant. For a brief shining moment it had seemed that she'd been offered a second chance, not just with her sister, but with Ivo. Life, however, wasn't that simple.

She'd never forgive herself for what she'd done to Ivo, for overriding his natural reserve, common sense, with a promise of something that was not hers to give.

Wanting it all.

She, more than anyone, should know how impossible that was. She'd found her sister. Eventually she'd find herself. And Ivo would, now the barriers had been broken down, find someone else.

Now, like her sister, she needed to live with what she'd done, move on, and she walked along the dress rail, running a finger over the hangers.

She'd cleared out a lot of her clothes, sent them to a charity shop. She was already building a new wardrobe for the different woman she was becoming and had only kept those that she needed for work, the ones that meant something special to her.

Her finger stopped at random and she took the dress from the rail, held it up for Daisy, hanging back in the doorway, to see. It was black, a sizzling strapless gown. She'd never wear it again. Had kept it out of sentimentality.

'I wore this dress to my first awards dinner years ago,' she said. Remembering the night. How nervous she'd been. How startled she'd been when she'd seen the glamorous photographs in the gossip mags the following week. Thinking it couldn't be her. It wasn't *her*… She turned to look at her sister. 'I wasn't nominated for anything. I was just a B-list celebrity there to make up the numbers. I can remember waiting for someone to call me on it. Ask me what the heck I thought I was doing there.'

She picked up the scissors, still lying where they'd fallen, gouging a lump out of the surface of the dressing table, and hacked it in two, discarding the pieces so that they fell to the floor to lie with the shreds of cream and gold. Ignored Daisy's gasp of horror as she continued running her finger along the rail.

'Now this one,' she said matter-of-factly, picking out a low-cut scarlet gown, 'was the dress I wore to some fancy affair involving bankers.'

Newly married, she'd been planning to wear something sedate in black, but then Manda had stuck her oar in, warning her not to make an exhibition of herself and what was a girl to do? Ivo hadn't said a word. His eyes had done the talking and, later, his fingers had done the walking.

'Billionaires, Daisy, drool just like normal men.'

Her sister whimpered as the scissors flashed and it joined the black dress on the floor.

Moving on.

She worked her way along the rail, picking out special favourites from these treasured gowns, recalling for her sister the special occasions on which she'd worn them. Birthdays, anniversaries, galas. Shutting her mind against the afterwards, when Ivo had unzipped, unhooked, unbuttoned each one, sometimes slowly, sometimes impatiently, always with passion.

By the time she reached the end of the rail Daisy was in tears and she was very close to them, her eyes swimming as she reached for the last gown.

A simple pleated column of grey silk, it was the first vintage gown she'd bought. Chanel at her most perfect. It was the gown she'd been wearing on that evening in the Serpentine Gallery.

Cutting this one would be hardest of all and yet it would be a symbol, a promise to her sister, even though it was one that Daisy would not understand. A promise to her sister, a demonstration that none of this mattered. That nothing would come between them ever again.

As she raised the scissors, Daisy caught her arm.

'Don't,' she sobbed. 'Please don't.' Then she sank to her knees, picking up tiny pieces of gold lace, holding them together as if she could undo the destruction. 'I'm sorry, Bella. So sorry.'

'It's only a dress, Daisy,' she said, letting the scissors fall to her side, almost faint with relief, sinking down beside her. 'It's not important. I just wanted you to understand that there is nothing more important to me than you.' She lifted her chin, forcing Daisy to look at her. 'You do believe me?'

'You looked like a princess that night,' she said, wiping her cheek with the palm of her hand. 'I was in the crowd outside the hotel, waiting for you to arrive. I wasn't going to ever come to you, mess up your life, but I wanted to see you and when you got out of the car everyone just sighed.'

'I was shaking with nerves.'

'Shaking? No! You were so beautiful. So perfect. And then you looked right at me and blew a kiss. Silly, you didn't know I was there…'

'I was thinking of you.'

She looked up. 'Were you?'

And Ivo…

No. She wouldn't, mustn't think of him. She'd never forgive herself for what she'd done to him, but he was a man. Strong. He'd be hurting, she knew that, but he'd survive without her.

Daisy would not.

'I thought you might be watching,' she said, pushing the thoughts away, concentrating on the girl in front of her. The future. 'I hoped, if you were, that you'd know it was just for you.'

'I should have trusted you. I thought…'

'I know what you thought. I let you down, wasn't there when you really needed me, but that will never happen again. Whatever happens, whatever you do, I will love you, be there for you.' Then, 'Tomorrow we'll see about getting a headstone for your Dad, hmm?'

For a minute they held each other, clinging on to each other amidst the wreckage of their lives, and Belle knew that a crisis had passed. Not the last crisis, but perhaps the biggest.

Ivo stayed at home to watch Belle's last morning. Every minute of it: the news, the papers, a celebrity interview, a fifty-year-old cab driver who'd written a book, a woman with cancer who was campaigning for some new treatment, the weather.

All the usual ingredients, Belle the glue that held it all together with her warmth, her charm, a little touch of steel that he'd somehow overlooked. Or maybe that was new. Something she'd found in the Himalayas. Something that made him love her all the more. He just hoped her wretched sister understood how lucky she was.

Today, her last day, the editors had put together a montage of her 'best bits' to end the programme. Her famous 'telethon' moment of discovery. Her first day on the set, making a hash of the weather. An interview that had gone hilariously wrong. Belle, eyes wide with excitement, at the wheel of a double-decker bus on the skid pad.

There was a shot of her interviewing the Director of the United Nations too. One of her with a much loved actor a few weeks before he died. That report to camera from the Himalayas with blood trickling down her face.

He'd expected it to end there with the credits rolling over that image, but instead the camera focused on her again.

Belle had a rare stillness, a presence in front of the camera, but today there was something new, something more. A maturity that had nothing to do with her grown-up haircut, more casual clothes. She had, he realised, finally learned to believe in herself and, despite everything, he found himself smiling. Urging her on to new heights, new challenges...

'I've been part of this programme one way and another for nine years,' she began, 'and, despite what you've just seen, the one thing I've learned is that it's not about me, but about you, the people who take time to tune in each busy morning, whether for a few minutes or an hour. It's about you, your lives, your news.' The camera went in close. 'Today, as you all know, is my last day on this sofa so I'm going to beg your indulgence and use these last few minutes to talk about myself.' She smiled. 'Actually, not just about me. I'm going to tell you the story of two little girls...'

He stood and watched as she told the world the story of her life. Of the horrors, but of the love too. And of a sister who she'd lost and had now found.

As she finished, she turned to smile at someone and the camera pulled back to reveal Daisy sitting beside her, sharing her sofa. Skinny as she was, lacking her sister's curves, she looked, at first glance, amazingly like Belle the day she'd smiled uncertainly up into a handheld camera. No doubt the studio make-up had emphasised the similarities and yet there was something...

For a moment there was complete silence and then the entire crew walked into the shot, applauding Belle, hugging them both.

He couldn't take his eyes off her, even when the door opened and Manda joined him. 'I've been watching next door. She's pretty amazing, your Belle, isn't she?'

'Not mine.'

Only for a few unforgettable moments yesterday afternoon, when the truth had set them free. When they'd used words that had been locked away.

Until the day he died he'd remember that moment when, poised above him, she'd kissed him, said, 'I love you…' before taking him to a place he'd only dreamed of. *Not his…*

'But yes, she is amazing,' he managed, through a throat aching so much that he could scarcely swallow.

'I was so sure she'd hurt you. I thought…' He put out a hand to stop her, but she shook her head, refusing to be silenced. 'I thought all she wanted was your money, but it wasn't like that, was it?'

'No,' he admitted. 'It wasn't anything like that.'

'Don't let her go, Ivo.'

'Her sister needs her more than I do right now.'

'Maybe she does, but Belle will need you too. We all need someone, a rock to cling to when things are bad.' She leaned against him. 'Or, in your case, a damn great cliff face.' Then, when he didn't respond, 'Her sister will move on, Ivo. Make a life of her own.'

'Eventually.' It didn't matter. Next week, next year, next life, he'd be there, if Belle should need him. Always be there.

Somehow he doubted that she would.

'What's she going to do, do you know?' Then, 'What can she do? The sister.'

'Daisy? I've no idea.' He turned to her, remembering his promise. 'Actually, I did tell Belle that you might give her a job.'

'Thanks for that.' Her standard response when he dumped some tedious job in her lap. He managed a grin, but she shook her head. 'No, I mean it, Ivo. Really. Thank you. For believing in me. Taking care of me. Saving me…' And suddenly his spiky, sharp little sister was the one struggling with words. 'I'll talk to her. Find out what she'd like to do.'

'She's fragile,' he warned.

'I won't break her; in fact she might find it easier to talk to me than Belle.' She glanced back towards the television set, where Belle, holding flowers that someone had thrust into her arms, was smiling into the camera as the credits rolled. 'What about Belle? What's she going to do?'

'I've no idea. She did have an idea for a documentary on adoption and I suggested she form her own production company.'

'That's not really her thing, is it?' Then, 'I can't see her heading up a media company. But maybe there is something she could do.'

'Leave it, Manda,' he warned.

'I hear what you say, Ivo, but are you saying "leave it" because you don't want me involved? Or are you warning me off because you can rely on me to do the exact opposite of what you say?'

'You've grown out of that nonsense.'

'Have I?'

'Don't be clever.'

'I just can't help it.' Then, 'I'll have a little chat with Daisy first, I think. But not just yet. I'll wait a week or two. Give them time to get bored playing happy families.' Then, 'Don't mess things up by sending her flowers or supportive little emails, will you?'

'If you're playing reverse psychology, you've picked the wrong man,' he said.

No flowers. No emails.

Just emptiness.

CHAPTER ELEVEN

BELLE began, quite irrationally, to hate the doorbell. Not because of who it might be —network people, her agent, who didn't seem to understand the word 'no'—but because of who it wasn't.

Just how stupid could one woman be?

First she'd left Ivo and then, when he'd bared his soul, admitted that he'd been prepared to compromise his own desperate decision, overcome his own fears to give her what she wanted, she'd sent him away. Rejected him, put her sister first. Made it clear that he came second.

No man was going to stand for that, come back for more. Especially not a man like Ivo Grenville.

She picked up the entry phone. 'Yes?'

'It's Miranda, Belle. Can I come up?'

She buzzed her in. His sister was no substitute, but she'd breathed the same air, talked to him, could tell her how he was…

'Great sofa,' Manda said, sweeping into the room in a dramatic swirl of the season's most cutting-edge style, a whisper of some rare scent, picking out the one thing that she hadn't chosen. 'Very eye-catching.'

Oh, right. She was being sarcastic.

'Ivo said your flat had a certain appeal.'

'Really?' What else had he said…?

'I have to confess, I thought his view was coloured by lust but actually he's right. Of course what you really need is to completely restore the house, turn it back into a family home. Maybe convert the lower ground floor into a garden flat for Daisy. So much more suitable for a pram,' she said.

'What can I do for you, Miranda?' Belle enquired sharply, refusing to be drawn into whatever game she thought she was playing.

'Nothing. It's your sister I've come to see. I understand she's in the market for a job.' She didn't wait for an answer but, turning to Daisy, said, 'I saw you on television last month. You've got your sister's smile.' Before Daisy had time to demonstrate it, she continued, 'I have no doubt that the rest of you will catch up in time. Motherhood can do wonders, I understand.' She extended her hand. 'I'm Manda Grenville, Ivo's sister.'

'Ivan the Terrible *and* Cruella de Ville,' Daisy replied, ignoring it. 'A neat match.'

Manda's eyes widened slightly and then, even as Belle held her breath, she threw back her head and laughed. 'The buxom Belle but with an edge. Brilliant. We're going to get along just fine.'

Infuriating though it was, it seemed that they did, perhaps recognising something in one another. And Belle had to admit that the job offer was good news. She hadn't expected Ivo to remember. She should have given him more credit; he might be hurt, but he wouldn't take his feelings out on Daisy.

She had tried to talk to her sister about the future; she was quick, clever, could easily get a place at college. She'd refused to even discuss it with her.

'Is there any hope of a cup of coffee, Belle?' Miranda asked.

About to remind her that if she wanted coffee she knew where the nearest deli was, she held her tongue, glad to have her as an ally on her sister's behalf, even if she'd never been a friend to her.

'Of course. Daisy? Can I get you anything?'

'Is there any of that honey and camomile tea left?'

She boiled the kettle, took the coffee from the fridge and spooned some into the cafetière; wrinkling up her nose at the smell, she decided to join Daisy in a cup of herb tea.

Daisy and Manda were, unlikely as that seemed, deep in conversation when she carried through the tray. She turned down the heating, then opened the French windows.

'Good grief, Bella, do you want us to freeze in here?'

'It's so stuffy in here,' she said. Then, realising that they were both staring at her, 'Maybe I'm coming down with something.'

'It must be something going around,' Manda said pointedly. 'Ivo has matching symptoms.'

'He's not well?'

'Nothing that a decent night's sleep wouldn't fix. Why don't you go and have a lie down?'

'I'm fine, really,' she began. Then, as Manda poured out the coffee and the smell reached her, she realised that was not the case and had to make a run for the bathroom, only just making it before she threw up.

She refused to let Daisy or Manda make a fuss, waving them away. 'It's just some bug. I'll lie down for a minute.'

Manda was still there when she emerged an hour later, slightly fuzzy from a nap and starving hungry.

'Is that pizza…?'

'We sent out for it. Daisy's choice.'

'Bliss. Did she leave any anchovies?'

'What is it with the pair of you and anchovies?' Manda demanded as Belle, spotting one that had been overlooked, picked it off and ate it.

'Belle!' Daisy protested. 'You hate anchovies.'

'I just fancied something salty.' She licked the tip of her thumb. 'What?'

They shook their heads as one and Manda quickly said, 'I'm glad you're back with us. Daisy and I are all sorted. All we need now is you.'

'Me?'

'It's this kids' charity thing I've got involved with. It seems to have been provoked by the huge response to your coverage of the charity bike ride. There's been a bit of a popular outcry and politicians are feeling bruised by the criticism. Things need to be done. The question is what things.'

'You'd like me to give you a list?'

'I was hoping for rather more than that, to be honest. A picture being, as we both know, worth a thousand words, what I need is someone to take a camera crew and show the world just how bad things are. An ambassador for the street kids, if you like. With your credentials, you appear to be the obvious choice.'

Daisy's face was glowing with excitement. 'Manda wants me to go with her on a pre-filming recce. As her assistant.'

'You're pregnant, Daisy.'

'Well, duh! This is the twenty-first century; I don't have to stay at home in purdah. It'll be during the middle three months.' Her voice was pleading. 'We're going to South America, the Far East...'

'I'll take care of her, Belle.'

'Will you?' Then, because she had to ask, 'Was this your idea?'

'You think Ivo is behind it? I promise you, he expressively forbade me from asking for your help.'

'Oh.' Belle felt like a tyre with the air let out. It was like the doorbell, she thought. She understood that it couldn't possibly be him, but she would keep hoping...

'Please, Belle!' Daisy begged. 'Please say you'll do it.'

She weighed up the options. Daisy, sulking and miserable under her feet day and night. Or with an exciting job, a future.

And not just Daisy. This was a new chance for her to do something important. Something that would make a difference.

'I guess you'd better go to the Post Office and pick up a passport application form,' she said.

'You saw her? How is she?'

Ivo might have tried to discourage his sister from whatever scheme she was hatching, but he'd been pacing the library, waiting for her to come home.

'Feeling a little under the weather, if you really want to know.' Manda settled on the sofa and put her feet up. 'Some tedious little bug, no doubt. It's that time of year.' Then, 'You're right about her flat, by the way. It's charming. Shame about the sofa.' She tilted her head to look at him. 'Did you know that there's one just like it for sale on the next floor?'

'The sofa?'

'Her flat.'

'Not any more.'

She swivelled round. 'You've bought it? When did you organise that?'

'I put in an offer the Monday after Belle left me.'

'Really? Does she know?'

'Not yet.' Then, 'You might as well know that I've bought the other two flats as well. I now own the entire house except the top floor.'

She wrinkled her brow in a thoughtful frown. 'All the flats were for sale at the same time?'

'If you offer enough money, anything is for sale.'

'And your plan is?'

'Shot to pieces, if you really want to know.'

'Oh, I don't know. Once I've whisked Daisy Dreadful off to South America the coast will be clear. You can move in downstairs and lay siege to the fair lady. Ply her with pizza. Just make sure to specify extra anchovies.'

'She hates anchovies.'

'Yes. Interesting.' Then, 'Whatever. Just think about it.'

'What on earth is going on downstairs?' Belle demanded.

The noise was driving her mad. No. Everything was driving her mad. The fact that her perfect minimalist flat had been taken over by the Christmas fairy in the shape of Daisy. That everything capable of carrying a decoration had been lit, baubled and tinselled.

That the freezer was full to the brim with food that made her ill just to think of it.

That all she wanted to do was lie down in a darkened room until the whole thing was over.

'The ground floor tenants are moving out today,' Daisy said. 'They've bought some swanky place in Bankside, apparently.'

'That's the whole place empty except for us? Does everyone

else know something I don't?' Then, as Daisy placed a beautifully gift-wrapped package in front of her, 'What's this?'

'An early Christmas present. Something I think you might find a use for.'

She eased herself up into a sitting position, told herself not to be such a Grinch—Daisy deserved this Christmas—and made herself smile. 'That's so sweet. Thank you.' She kissed her sister, undid the blue bow, loosened the silver wrapping paper. Frowned in confusion as she looked at the box in her hand. Then thought for a moment that she was going to be sick again. 'Is this a joke?'

'No, it's a pregnancy test kit. The latest high-tech job. No little blue lines or crosses on this one. It actually says "Pregnant" or "Not Pregnant". How neat is that?' Daisy said, totally pleased with herself.

Belle swallowed. Not neat at all.

'I'm not pregnant,' she said.

'You're sick all the time,' Daisy said, shifting all her weight to one leg, sticking out her hip and ticking off her counter-arguments on her fingers, one by one. 'The kitchen cupboard is stacked with cans of anchovies as if you're afraid they're about to go extinct. You go green if I mention coffee. And yesterday I caught you eating a pickled cucumber out of the jar. Two months ago that was me.' Then, pulling a face, 'Except for the pickle.'

'I like pickled cucumbers.'

'Are your breasts tender?' she persisted. 'I have noticed that you're wearing your softest bras.'

'Well, maybe, but—'

'But nothing. Quit with the excuses. It's time you stopped hiding from the truth and admitted you're up the duff. In the club. That there is, in the vernacular, a bun in your oven.'

Vernacular? She'd been spending way too much time with Manda.

'No, darling,' she said, pushing her lank fringe back from her forehead with a shaking hand. 'You don't understand. I can't possibly be pregnant.'

'You're doing a very good impression of it.'

'It's just a bug. Something I picked up when I was abroad.'

'They do the delayed action kind now?'

'Please!' she begged. 'I can't... Ivo can't...'

'What?'

'He can't have children.' Daisy did not look convinced. 'He had a vasectomy.'

'Is that a fact? So who's been a naughty girl, then?'

'No!'

'I was kidding, Bella.' Daisy placed the box in her hands, eased her to her feet. 'The bathroom is that way. Do you want me to come and read the instructions for you?'

'This is ridiculous.'

'Really? So prove it.'

Belle sat on the edge of the bath staring at the little wand she was holding. The single word.

'Pregnant'

Around her, the world went about its business, unheeding. The bumping and shouting as the removal men shifted furniture.

An impatient motorist hooted.

A child cried.

A brass band in the market was playing a Christmas carol.

'Bella?' Daisy's voice was no longer teasing but anxious. 'Bella, can I come in?' She didn't wait, but opened the door. Took the stick from her hand. 'I really hate to say I told you so...'

'It's wrong.'

'Oh, Bella...' Daisy put her arms around her. 'It's okay.'

'No. No, it's not. It can't be true,' she said. She wanted it to be true. Longed for it to be true. But it couldn't be. 'It would take a miracle.'

Ivo had begged for one. For her sake, she reminded herself. Nothing had changed for him.

'Maybe it's a dud,' Daisy offered gently, as if she were talking to a child. She didn't understand. Couldn't know... 'Why don't I go and get another kit? A different kind.'

'Whatever it takes to convince you.'

An hour later they were surrounded by empty cartons, the little sticks they'd contained, each one telling her, with blue lines, pink lines, blue crosses, the same thing.

Pregnant. Pregnant. Pregnant.

'There's one more,' Daisy said.

'I couldn't squeeze out another drop.'

'So what? You're ready to accept that they're right?' Then, misunderstanding, 'It's not so bad, you know. And our kids will be almost like twins.'

'You don't understand.'

'Maybe I do.' Daisy knelt in front of her. 'It's okay, really.' Then, '*I'm* going to be okay. Selfish. A brat. Afraid that you'd get tired of me. But you sent him away for me, didn't you? Even though you love him.'

'No!'

'Then why hasn't he been to see you?'

'He's busy.'

'He hasn't even called you.'

Belle, unable to speak, just shook her head.

'I'm off to South America after Christmas,' Daisy said, 'but I don't think I can go if you're going to be on your own.'

'Don't be silly. I'll be fine.'

'I don't think you will. No. That's the deal. Call him or Manda will have to find someone else to run her errands.'

'Daisy…' She reached out, caught her hand. 'You know I'd never let you down, don't you? That I'll always been here for you.'

'Yes, Bella, I know.' Then, leaping to her feet, 'Well, what are you waiting for? Call Ivan the Terrible, tell him that, snip or not, he's about to become a daddy.'

Ivo had used work, from his earliest days at school, to block out the emptiness in his life. For the first time in his life it wasn't working.

He'd stopped going into the office, had abandoned ongoing projects to his more than capable deputies, who were doubtless delighted at the chance to show what they could do, using the excuse that he needed to sort out the Camden house.

When he'd seen the flat below hers was for sale it had seemed as if it was meant. Quite what he was going to do with it he hadn't decided. But then Daisy had turned up and it had all seemed so simple. He'd convert the garden flat for Daisy. Move in between them. Be a friend. A father…

Stupid.

Now, the keys in his hand, the empty rooms mocking him, he wasn't able to rouse himself to care about anything very much.

His cellphone bleeped to warn him that he had a text message. His first reaction was to ignore it, but there were people relying on him, for whom he was responsible. He pulled it from his pocket, flipped it open. Stared at it. He hadn't thought his day could get any worse, but it just had.

There was a tap at the front door to the flat. 'It's probably the removal men wanting a cup of tea,' Belle said, drying her hair. 'Can you handle it?'

'No problem.'

She looked at her face in the mirror, pinched her cheeks to put a bit of colour in them. Put on a pair of earrings. Realised that everything had gone very quiet.

'Daisy?'

'Your sister said to tell you that she's meeting Manda for lunch.' Belle spun around on the stool. Ivo was standing in the doorway watching her. 'Your message said you wanted to see me. To talk about the future.'

For a moment she could hardly catch her breath, let alone speak. It had been just over a month and he looked no better than her. Gaunt, hollow-eyed…

'I only sent that text a few minutes ago.'

'I was in the flat downstairs.'

She frowned. 'But it's empty. It's been empty for weeks…'

'Not any more. I've been taking possession of my latest acquisition. What do you want to see me about, Belle? If it's—'

'The flat? You've bought the flat?'

'Actually, I've bought the whole house,' he said impatiently. 'All of it except this floor. Does it matter?'

'That depends on your reason. Are you going to move in?'

'Yes. No…' He shook his head. 'Belle, if you want to talk about a divorce—'

'What? No,' she said. 'No.' She turned and picked up a silk jewellery roll that was lying on the dressing table. Offered it to him. 'It's this.'

Ivo took it. 'What is it?'

'Open it and see.'

He shrugged, undid the tie, then placed it on the bed and rolled it open.

In each pocket there was a small plastic stick. Each one was slightly different. He'd never actually seen one before, but it didn't take a genius to work out what they were. What he didn't understand was what she was doing with them. Telling him. Until the last one. That said it in one simple word.

Pregnant.

He thought he knew pain, understood every way in which the heart could be wrenched open, torn apart, bleed. But in that moment, as the possibilities raced through his head, he learned different.

'Oh, my love…' Somehow he was on his knees and she had her arms around him, holding him, crushing him to her. 'What have you done?'

'Me?' She drew back a little.

'Was it a donor? Were you that desperate?'

'No… Don't you understand, Ivo?' She took the pregnancy test strip, knelt before him, holding it out. 'What this is, my love, is a miracle. You asked for one, remember? For me.' She lifted a hand, touched his cheek. 'It's your baby, Ivo. My baby. Our baby.'

He was swamped with confusion. 'Our baby? But…'

She laid a finger on his lips. 'I assumed, from what you said, that the doctor told you that your vasectomy was irreversible. That there was nothing to be done.'

'No. He did his best, but warned me he couldn't guarantee anything.'

'It would have stood a rather better chance if I hadn't been taking the pill for the last three years, don't you think?' she asked, smiling.

'But…' He stopped. 'No. You wanted a baby. Why would you take the pill?'

'I saw your face, Ivo. You didn't have to tell me that you didn't want children. I spent twenty-four hours after you left me alone on our honeymoon island coming to terms with that. At the end of it I chose you for as long as you wanted me. Not for your money. Not for the security. For no other reason than that I loved you.'

'I didn't know…'

She stopped him with a kiss. For a moment he had no thought but to take the blissful moment, forget anything else.

Later he said, 'You stopped taking the pill when you left?'

'Why would I need them? There wasn't anyone else I was planning to have sex with.' She smiled. 'To sleep with.'

'Keep it that way,' he said, then drew back a little, looking at her as if he still couldn't quite believe it. 'Our baby?'

'Ivo, children need parents who want them. Who can love them. I know this wasn't what you wanted. I want you to know that I can do this on my own.'

It was a question. She needed to know. Had a right to know.

'You don't have to do anything on your own ever again, Belle. You're right. This is a miracle. But the biggest miracle is not that you loved me enough to stay, but found the strength to leave. Forced me to acknowledge the truth. I love you, Belle Davenport, love the baby we made.' Then, 'Or are you telling me that I don't have a choice? That your sister still comes first.'

'It was Daisy who made me call you.'

Belle looked up as the brass band in the marketplace struck up 'Joy to the World'. Then she turned back to him. 'You've seen the decorations? I should warn you that she's planning a traditional old-fashioned family Christmas. How do you feel about that?'

'Here?'

'Could you bear it?'

'I could bear Christmas in a tent if it meant sharing it with you.' He laid his palm over her stomach. 'Both of you.'

'There's Daisy and Manda as well.'

'Maybe not a tent, in that case. I think perhaps I'd better get the flat downstairs furnished, just as a stopgap, or it's going to be a bit cramped.'

'A stopgap?'

'My plan was to restore the house to a family home, bit by bit. Make it so welcoming that you couldn't resist moving in.'

'What about the house in Belgravia?'

'Would you move back?'

'I'd rather take the tent.'

'Then it's history.'

'You're sure?'

'I've never been more certain of anything in my entire life. I just wish I could wipe out the last three years as easily, so that we could start again. Begin anew.'

'You really mean that?'

'With all my heart.'

They were still kneeling, face to face, and she took his hands in hers and said, 'I, Belinda Louise, take thee, Ivan George Michael, to my wedded husband. To have and to hold, from this day forward, for better, for worse, for richer for poorer, in sickness and in health, to love and to cherish, till death us do part...'

Her eyes filled as she said the words, tears flowing unchecked down her cheeks as Ivo followed her lead and reaffirmed the vow he'd made three years before.

'From this day forward,' he said again and tenderly, gently kissed her. 'Until the end of time.'

Once Christmas—starting with a trip to the midnight service to thank whoever was watching over them for giving them all so much—was over, Ivo and Belle had a blissful month alone, while Manda and Daisy took off for foreign parts to explore the possibilities for their film.

They spent it planning their new home together, relaxed in each other's company, discovering the simple pleasures of marriage for the first time. Cooking together, sleeping together, wak-

ing in each other's arms. Neither of them in a hurry to be anywhere else.

It was tough being apart while they did the filming, yet exhilarating too. Belle's new-found confidence had given her a
harder edge that had the media clamouring for more; by the time
she and Manda were helping Daisy through her delivery and she
was welcoming her new nephew into the world, it had already
garnered half a dozen nominations for an award.

On the night it won the first of them, Belle was panting
through her own contractions, Ivo at her side, calm, quietly supportive, even when she completely lost it at one point, told him
and anyone else who'd listen that she'd changed her mind about
having a baby.

He was totally in control until the moment his baby daughter
was delivered into his hands.

Then, tears streaming down his face, he was reduced to inco-
herent gratitude and joy as he laid their child in her arms.

'So small, so helpless. Like a kitten,' he said, when he was,
at last, able to speak.

'Maybe we should call her Minette.'

'You've been working on your French.' He smiled, kissed
them both. 'Welcome, Minette.' Then, when the midwife made
it clear that there were things she needed to do, 'Manda is waiting
for news. And Daisy.'

'Will you call Claire and Simone too? I promised. They said
no matter what time of day or night.'

'No problem. I want to tell the whole world that I'm a
father.' He kissed her forehead and said, 'Did I tell you today
that I love you?'

'With every piece of ice. Every damp cloth. When you mas-
saged my back.' She grinned up at him, 'When you agreed with
every word of the abuse I heaped on you.'

'It was all true.'

'Not all of it...' She took his hand, kissed his palm where her
nails had dug in, and then looked up, suddenly grave, 'Most of
all, my love, when you cried.' Then, 'Did I tell you?'

He looked down at his beloved wife, who was almost asleep.

'I promise you that there isn't a man on earth who feels more loved, more blessed, than I do at this moment,' he said, but softly, so as not to disturb her.

* * * * *

Welcome to cowboy country...

Turn the page for a sneak preview of
TEXAS BABY
by
Kathleen O'Brien
An exciting new title from Harlequin Superromance
for everyone who loves stories about the West.

Harlequin Superromance—
Where life and love weave together
in emotional and unforgettable ways.

CHAPTER ONE

CHASE TRANSFERRED his gaze to the road and identified a foreign spot on the horizon. A car. Almost half a mile away, where the straight, tree-lined drive met the public road. He could tell it was coming too fast, but judging the speed of a vehicle moving straight toward you was tricky.

It wasn't until it was about two hundred yards away that he realized the driver must be drunk...or crazy. Or both.

The guy was going maybe sixty. On a private drive, out here in ranch country, where kids or horses or tractors or stupid chickens might come darting out any minute, that was criminal. Chase straightened from his comfortable slouch and waved his hands.

"Slow down, you fool," he called out. He took the porch steps quickly and began walking fast down the driveway.

The car veered oddly, from one lane to another, then up onto the slight rise of the thick green spring grass. It just barely missed the fence.

"Slow down, damn it!"

He couldn't see the driver, and he didn't recognize this automobile. It was small and old, and couldn't have cost much even when it was new. It was probably white, but now it needed either a wash or a new paint job or both.

"Damn it, what's wrong with you?"

At the last minute, he had to jump away, because the idiot behind the wheel clearly wasn't going to turn to avoid a collision. He couldn't believe it. The car kept coming, finally slowing a little, but it was too late.

Still going about thirty miles an hour, it slammed into the large, white-brick pillar that marked the front boundaries of the house. The pillar wasn't going to give an inch, so the car had to. The front end folded up like a paper fan.

It seemed to take forever for the car to settle, as if the trauma happened in slow motion, reverberating from the front to the back of the car in ripples of destruction. The front windshield suddenly seemed to ice over with lethal bits of glassy frost. Then the side windows exploded.

The front driver's door wrenched open, as if the car wanted to expel its contents. Metal buckled hideously. Small pieces, like hubcaps and mirrors, skipped and ricocheted insanely across the oyster-shell driveway.

Finally, everything was still. Into the silence, a plume of steam shot up like a geyser, smelling of rust and heat. Its snake-like hiss almost smothered the low, agonized moan of the driver.

Chase's anger had disappeared. He didn't feel anything but a dull sense of disbelief. Things like this didn't happen in real life. Not in his life. Maybe the sun had actually put him to sleep….

But he was already kneeling beside the car. The driver was a woman. The frosty glass-ice of the windshield was dotted with small flecks of blood. She must have hit it with her head, because just below her hairline a red liquid was seeping out. He touched it. He tried to wipe it away before it reached her eyebrow, though, of course that made no sense at all. Her eyes were shut.

Was she conscious? Did he dare move her? Her dress was covered in glass, and the metal of the car was sticking out lethally in all the wrong places.

Then he remembered, with an intense relief, that every good medical man in the county was here, just behind the house, drinking his champagne. He found his phone and paged Trent.

The woman moaned again.

Alive, then. Thank God for that.

He saw Trent coming toward him, starting out at a lope, but quickly switching to a full run.

"Get Dr. Marchant," Chase called. "Don't bother with 911."

Trent didn't take long to assess the situation. A fraction of a second, and he began pulling out his cell phone and running toward the house.

The yelling seemed to have roused the woman. She opened her eyes. They were blue and clouded with pain and confusion.

"Chase," she said.

His breath stalled. His head pulled back. "What?"

Her only answer was another moan, and he wondered if he had imagined the word. He reached around her and put his arm behind her shoulders. She was tiny. Probably petite by nature, but surely way too thin. He could feel her shoulder blades pushing against her skin, as fragile as the wishbone in a turkey.

She seemed to have passed out, so he put his other arm under her knees and lifted her out. He tried to avoid the jagged metal, but her skirt caught on a piece and the tearing sound seemed to wake her again.

"No," she said. "Please."

"I'm just trying to help," he said. "It's going to be all right."

She seemed profoundly distressed. She wriggled in his arms, and she was so weak, like a broken bird. It made him feel too big and brutish. And intrusive. As if touching her this way, his bare hands against the warm skin behind her knees, were somehow a transgression.

He wished he could be more delicate. But he smelled gasoline, and he knew it wasn't safe to leave her here.

Finally he heard the sound of voices, as guests began to run around the side of the house, alerted by Trent. Dr. Marchant was at the front, racing toward them as if he were forty instead of seventy. Susannah was right behind him, her green dress floating around her trim legs.

"Please," the woman in his arms murmured again. She looked at him, the expression in her blue eyes lost and bewildered. He wondered if she might be on drugs. Hitting her head on the windshield might account for this unfocused, glazed look, but it couldn't explain the crazy driving.

"Please, put me down. Susannah… The wedding…"

Chase's arms tightened instinctively, and he froze in his tracks. She whimpered, and he realized he might be hurting her. "Say that again?"

"The wedding. I have to stop it."

* * * * *

Be sure to look for TEXAS BABY,
available September 11, 2007,
as well as other fantastic Superromance titles
available in September.

HARLEQUIN® *Super Romance*®

Welcome to Cowboy Country...

TEXAS BABY

by Kathleen O'Brien

#1441

Chase Clayton doesn't know what to think.
A beautiful stranger has just crashed his
engagement party, demanding that he not
marry because she's pregnant with his baby.
But the kicker is—he's never seen her before.

Look for TEXAS BABY and other fantastic
Superromance titles on sale September 2007.

Available wherever books are sold.

HARLEQUIN® *Super Romance*®

**Where life and love weave together
in emotional and unforgettable ways.**

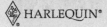

REQUEST YOUR FREE BOOKS!
2 FREE NOVELS PLUS 2
FREE GIFTS!

From the Heart, For the Heart

HR07

HARLEQUIN *Romance*

Coming Next Month

#3973 PROMOTED: NANNY TO WIFE Margaret Way

When dark, brooding Holt McMaster hires Marissa Devlin to be his daughter's new governess, Marissa's heart is quickly stolen by Holt's little girl…and by the magnificent cattle baron himself! Is it possible that the new nanny may also be the perfect wife?

#3974 THE BRIDAL CONTRACT Susan Fox
Western Weddings

Fay Sheridan is facing the bleakest moment of her life, but one man plucks her from despair and into safety…Chase Rafferty. Rugged rancher Chase knows that there is a fun-loving young woman hiding inside Fay, and he will do anything to see her start living again…even propose!

#3975 OUTBACK BOSS, CITY BRIDE Jessica Hart
Bridegroom Boss

Meredith has been forced to take a job on an Outback station with Hal Granger—a boss she can't stand! It should be easy to keep everything purely professional—except she can't stop thinking about what it would be like to kiss him! And Meredith's about to find out….

#3976 NEEDED: HER MR. RIGHT Barbara Hannay
Secrets We Keep

Simone is determined to deal with a dreadful secret she has kept, and move on with her life. Until her private diary is lost…and found by billionaire journalist Ryan Tanner. Simone is immediately suspicious of gorgeous Ryan, but he may just be her Mr. Right in a million….

#3977 THE ITALIAN SINGLE DAD Jennie Adams

Luchino Montichelli broke Bella's heart. Years on he has turned up in Australia with his young daughter. The brooding man who looks at his little girl with such tenderness is the Luc Bella fell in love with. But can she trust him enough to take another chance on this Italian single dad?

#3978 MARRIAGE AT CIRCLE M Donna Alward
Heart to Heart

Town sweetheart Grace Lundquist is determined to hide her pain. But try as she might to keep protective rancher Mike out of her business, Grace can't douse the spark between them. Except she will never be able to give him the one thing he really needs—a family to call his own….

HRCNM0807